CHASING THE WIND

Books by Bruce Coyle

The Glory Road (2017)

Far From Glory (2018)

Sawdust and Smoke (2022)

Chasing the Wind (2024)

ALTRO EDITION
FINNS WAY
B O O K S

a novel

Bruce Coyle

"You don't have anything
if you don't have the stories."

--Leslie Marmon Silko

CHASING THE WIND

1

The drive to the south jetty on Heron Bay took me across Table Bluff, passing by the old county dump. When I was a kid, I enjoyed going to the dump with my dad, tossing things over the bank, trying to hit "targets" at the bottom—an old toilet or a washing machine with the lid open. It made those trips to the dump a lot of fun.

Of course, the dump was closed now, filled in and sanitized—turned into a "transfer station" that was more friendly to the environment—giant metal containers set in the ground, to be lifted out and taken God knows where for disposal.

At the edge of the bluff, the road offered a fine view of the ocean and the strip of beach before it narrowed and turned into a series of switchbacks leading downhill to the south jetty beach. On a sunny day, it would have been pretty, some might say, but the morning was overcast and gloomy, and gathering clouds offshore promised rain.

When I got to the bottom of the hill, I could see the orange metal gate at the end of the road. The end of the road! When I was younger, the end of the road was a long way off, and there was usually a big "no trespassing" sign posted there. I'd climbed over a few of those gates to see what was on the other side, but I was an old man now. The end of the road wasn't very far off for me these days, and I knew damn well what was on the other side.

At any rate, the gate to the beach was open. I parked my car outside the gate and got out. I hadn't been here since I was a teenager, and a lot had changed. Back then the gate was always locked, the beach closed to the public.

Not long after the Second World War, there'd been a violent incident on the beach. A soldier who'd just gotten back home had driven out to the south jetty with his girlfriend for a little night time hanky-panky. Supposedly they were attacked by a person or persons unknown. The soldier was beaten pretty badly, left for dead, and the girl was nowhere to be found. The sheriff suspected the young man at first, but his injuries suggested that he wasn't responsible for what happened. They never found the girl, though.

They closed the beach after that, put up that big metal gate with the no trespassing sign. For years no one visited the south jetty beach. Parents told their kids about what happened there and warned them to stay away. Little kids were frightened by spooky stuff like that, but older teenagers, including me, sometimes drove out to that beach to test the waters for themselves.

But that was fifty years ago, and only old farts like me remember what happened here back then. Nowadays it's all about public access, and opening the beaches to give the tree huggers a chance to dip their toes in the Pacific.

Well, there isn't much to see here. The beach is just a long, featureless strip of sand between the ocean and the marshy end of the bay. Salmon Creek makes its way into the bay at this end, but decades of logging have plugged the creek with debris, and the salmon can't find their way back anymore. An abandoned dredge lists off kilter at the edge of the marsh. The beaches north of the bay are a lot more interesting, with tide pools to explore and sea stacks offshore.

The north jetty is a different story. The lumber mills took hold over there long ago. Used to be a lot of pine trees growing all over. People could go over and cut one for Christmas, but of course they're all gone now, the land covered over by rundown company houses. Used to be a lot of tepee burners, too, spewing out smoke from burning wood waste. Now they're all gone, replaced by the new pulp mill.

They stopped burning the wood waste, figured out how to make other things out of it. Supposed to be another environmentally friendly move. Got something called a Cottrell precipitator that removes dust particles from the waste gases and keeps them out of the air. Of course that gunk has to go somewhere, so they pump it into the ocean through a giant pipe. The air is cleaner, but ever since the pulp mill started up, there's a sour smell in the air that travels for miles. It was the first thing I noticed when I got out of the car.

I didn't see anybody else around—no hikers when I looked down the beach, no cars parked nearby. That was fine with me. I was comfortable being by myself. I don't think I'm very good company anymore. Besides, I was here to try out my new toy. I walked around to the back of the car and unlocked the trunk.

When I reached for the handle to lift the lid, I thought of my first trip to the south jetty. I had that '39 Chevy I'd rescued from Mrs. Palmrose's garage. It was the Master Deluxe, the one with the clamshell trunk and the big headlights on the fenders. Quite a car, that one, lots of character. Not like these lookalike matchboxes everybody drives nowadays. Wish I still had that car. The old stovebolt six purred like a kitten. Squirrel and I had a lot of fun in that Chevy.

Boy, am I stuck in the past! Seems like all I think about these days. Of course, when I was a kid, I didn't have much of a past to think about, but now it seems that's all I do. Things keep changing, and all those changes make me uneasy. I liked things the way they were, but everything's different now. I'm different—a sour old crosspatch most of the time. Maybe that happens to everyone if they live long enough.

Her name was Sorrel, but the kids teased her, calling her Squirrel, and the name stuck after a while. She had dark red hair and blue eyes that dazzled me. We came out here in the evening that time. We had a picnic basket in the trunk and a couple of blankets to spread out on the sand. We gathered some driftwood, built a fire, and watched the sun go down, cuddling together with one of the blankets wrapped around us.

When it was dark, we gathered our things, kicked sand on the fire, and headed back to the car. We fooled around in the car for a while, steaming up the windows in the old Chevy. I remember how she said, "Ohh… Billy!" in that most amazing way. I had to wipe the windshield before I could see well enough to drive. Funny thing to remember, that. I wonder if Squirrel would remember that kind of thing. Guys always remember stuff like that—who they were with, what they did. Most guys I knew could make you a list. Maybe we all get mired in the past when the end of the road is staring us in the face.

Well, I'd found something new to do. I had a new toy to play with, a metal detector the guy at the sporting goods store talked me into buying. "Minelab Explorer SE Pro—top of the line, let me tell you!" And then he proceeded to tell me about all the stuff he and his kids found on playgrounds and beaches. The new models were coming out, so this one was on sale. "A real bargain," he said. He was quite a talker. After a while, I was willing to buy the thing just to get out of the store.

I pulled my "SE Pro" out of the trunk and slammed the lid. I plopped my old fishing hat on my head and headed along the spit toward the south jetty. The clouds offshore were starting to look ominous, but I thought the rain would hold off for a while. The wind had picked up and the seagulls wheeling overhead were drifting inland. Determined to try out my new toy, I zipped my jacket, turned up the collar, and marched through the dune grass and down to the shore.

I powered up my new toy. The directions promised an "easy learning curve" in Quickstart Mode, with "Full Band Spectrum multiple frequency technology," whatever that meant. I figured even an old dog like me could learn a new trick if he tried.

I plodded along in the soft sand, listening for the boops and beeps that would tell me I'd found hidden treasure. I walked for a while, hearing nothing but the booming surf and, once, the far-off lunchtime horn at one of the mills on the north side of the bay.

When I got to the end of the jetty and looked across the entrance to the bay, I could see the pulp mill with the white smoke streaming up from the enormous stack, flattening on the wind and drifting south over the town of Buck's Landing. The sour smell washed over me like memories.

As I started back down the beach toward the car, I was treated to a few beeps and boops from the metal detector. I managed to dig up a few pull tabs from old soda cans. Whoever dreamed up those things should have been fired. Just try stepping on one of those things with bare feet and you'll know what I mean. At least nowadays the tabs stay on the can.

I found a couple of coins, a Roosevelt dime, a couple of nickels, and best of all, an Indian head penny. I hadn't seen one of those in years. I don't collect coins or anything, but I remember getting one of those now and then in change when I was a kid. Just another reminder of how old I am.

I was climbing the dunes to get to the car when there was a high-pitched beep from the metal detector. There was a steep cut in the dunes here. Before the loggers plugged up the creek, the water used to flow around the end of the bay and across the beach, emptying into the sea. But the water was just a trickle now and only fed that marsh, as what was left of the stream drained into the bay. That old dredge was mute testimony to some feeble efforts to keep the creek flowing.

The cut in the dunes was all that was left of the old streambed. I waved the search coil at the end of the shaft here and there, trying to pinpoint the location of whatever my detector had located. It was a higher-pitched beep, which was supposed to be a sign of something better than a low-value metal like iron, which produced a dull beep. I had enough rusty nails at home, so I was kind of excited by the thought of finding something good.

It was starting to rain, but I kept at it. The car wasn't very far away, and I wanted to see what I'd discovered. The sound was strongest at a spot on the bank of the old streambed, a couple of feet off the bottom. I found a long piece of driftwood about the right size and started poking around in the dirt. After a few attempts at loosening the dirt, a chunk fell out and rolled down the slope to the streambed. The chunk of dirt and rock fell apart when it hit the bottom. When I picked through the pieces, I found something shiny embedded in the dirt.

It was starting to pour now. Water was running off the brim of my hat and down the back of my neck. Puddles in the streambed were turning into little trickles heading toward the sea. I rubbed that shiny thing between my palms to get a better look.

It was a little box, silver maybe. There was something on the top—a design, maybe some writing. I was getting soaked. I had to get out of the rain. I stuffed it in my pocket with the coins I'd found and made a dash for the car, struggling up the bank to get to the top of the dune.

I stowed the metal detector in the trunk and hopped in the car to get out of the rain. The windows fogged up as I settled in, but I started the engine and hit the switch for the defroster. Not like my old Chevy for sure. Could have used that back in the day when Squirrel and I were steaming up the windows. Now I was just a wet dog getting in out of the rain. My steam had cooled long ago.

When the windows cleared, I fastened the seat belt and headed back to the top of Table Bluff. The windshield wipers kept up a steady beat as they scrubbed back and forth. Not like the old Master Deluxe with the vacuum wipers that slowed down when you accelerated up a hill and then speeded up when you let off on the gas going down the other side.

The new wipers were steady and reliable, but not as entertaining. Some things changed for the better, I supposed. The old cars just had more character. I missed hearing that second gear whine as my Chevy lumbered up the steep hills. Driving felt more like flying by the seat of your pants back then.

Cars nowadays practically drive themselves, got automatic transmissions and "cruise control." Kids don't know what the clutch is for. Dial telephones and typewriters, too—relics from the past—like grumpy old farts like me.

It's not all sunshine and lollipops nowadays, and the gloomy weather always seems to put me in a funk, makes me think of what used to be and is no more. Folks talk about the "good ol' days," but they weren't always as good as they say. Still, we had all that youthful vigor and optimism, and the future we were headed for was filled with endless possibilities. We didn't know who we would become, but we were slowly turning into ourselves, one day at a time.

As I came down off Table Bluff, the road passed through

some bottom land before it joined the highway, lots of cows in the pastures beside white-painted barns. They weren't worried about the rain, making me think of that old ad for Carnation Condensed Milk, the "milk from contented cows." Only someone my age would remember that.

2

Driving up the narrow road with its twists and turns, I tried to avoid the ruts and washouts, afraid my car would bottom out and tear something loose. The old cars had a lot more ground clearance. That made me think of driving the old logging roads with my friend Pepper Woods.

Pepper lived down the road not far from my house, and we hung out together, especially in the summer. He was a couple of months younger, which put us in different grades, and during the school year he mostly palled around with the town kids. But in the summer, we spent a lot of time together. His folks had a small farm, and there was always a lot to do at Pepper's place. I helped him with the milk cows and learned how to drive a tractor and bale hay. We hiked all over and explored what we called the "ghost town," an abandoned lumber mill just up the road.

When Pepper was cutting hay for a guy named Willis Baker, he saw an old Model A Ford behind Willis' barn. That car looked pretty far gone to me, but Pepper bought it anyway. He towed it home, got it running, and we drove it all over the back roads that summer. Pepper wasn't old enough to get his license yet, but that didn't stop him.

He almost got stopped permanently when a logging truck clipped that car on a tight turn. Pepper put the car up against the bank at the edge of the road, but the tail end of the truck tore up the rear fender of the Model A. That near miss put the fear of God in Pepper for a week or so, but he didn't back down easily. Pepper liked to dance a lot closer to the fire than I did, but he often talked me into going along on his adventures.

Pepper was determined to replace his damaged fender with one from a car he'd seen in one of the buildings in that ghost town up the road. They'd started logging up there again, and everything was off limits, but Pepper was set on getting that fender. We ended up unraveling an old mystery that had haunted that place for years, but Pepper never did get that fender he wanted.

Things changed between us after that. Pepper and I went our separate ways. Pepper seldom rode the school bus anymore. He drove to school with Earlene most days. She was an Indian girl who lived back in the hills with her father, Ollie Mack. She'd had a crush on Pepper as long as I'd known her. I was still riding the bus to school, but I'd met Squirrel by then and when she was sitting beside me in the morning, I didn't mind taking the bus at all.

Roscoe Stapp had been the owner of that lumber camp. He'd vanished without a trace back in the early forties, before the war started. Turned out he'd stolen money from his two partners and they killed him when they found out what he'd done. Rooting through the old place, Pepper and I'd found evidence to prove it. When we showed the sheriff what we'd found, the two got hauled off to jail.

Those men had me scared stiff. One of them came to my house and threatened me when he found out I'd been poking around the old mill. Pepper was upset, too, but mostly 'cause he couldn't get the fender he wanted. Pepper was never really afraid of anything.

I wasn't really surprised when Pepper joined the army right out of high school. I was in my first year of college, ducking the draft with my II-S deferment, hoping the Vietnam War would end before I graduated. But Pepper didn't wait around to get drafted. He signed up soon after school was out. When I heard what he'd done, I figured it was just another one of his adventures, but I was pretty glad he hadn't roped me into that one.

A year or so later, Pepper's folks got the news that Pepper was MIA—missing in action. It was a shock, but they were still hopeful for his return. We all were, especially Earlene.

The old two lane was now a four-lane freeway connecting Buck's Landing with nearby towns. I was still thinking of Earlene and Pepper when I passed by the turnoff for the Indian casino on the Prairie Creek Rancheria. Earlene had kept her torch burning for Pepper for years after he was declared MIA. When Ollie passed away, she put away the past and embraced her heritage.

Earlene and her father had their own place, a little farm nowhere near any reservation, but Ollie had passed on what he knew of their ancestors' Yurok history. Earlene had tried to become a recognized tribal member, but it was a cumbersome process. She didn't need a paper from the government to prove what she knew in her heart. Her heart wasn't made of paper. She knew who she was when she looked in the mirror.

Earlene got a job at the casino, and got involved in Native issues. I'd seen her on television taking part in a demonstration over fishing rights up north on the Klamath River. She was in the thick of it, carrying a sign and chanting with the other protesters. She wore her pretty black hair in a single braid, trailing down her back, but there was a lot of gray in it now. She had given up on Pepper and had a new torch to carry. I was happy for her.

The skies over the bay began to clear as I followed the highway back toward Buck's Landing. I was ready to go home. My spirits always lifted when the sun came out. Squirrel knows when I'm in a funk I'm not fit to live with. Most of the time she tells me I need to get out on my own. "Go for a drive, Billy. Take a walk, just get out there and blow the stink off."

When I turned off the highway and crossed the bridge over the slough, I could see our place ahead on Prairie Creek Bottoms. There was a rainbow over our house. I knew Squirrel was at the end of the rainbow. She'd always been there.

3

The old farmhouse looked fresh and clean after the rain. The white two-story house with its wraparound porch was almost a hundred years old, but Russell Posey, Squirrel's father, had taken good care of it. The windmill beside the tankhouse turned lazily in the breeze, though it didn't really do anything but add character to the Posey farm. Russ had installed an electric pump with a pressure tank that boosted the old gravity-fed water supply from the wooden tank on top of the tankhouse. Like me, he liked to keep things the way they were, and he kept the windmill because it had always been there.

My folks had lived in a newer house further along Prairie Creek, near the abandoned lumber mill. Our parents were gone now. We had sold my folks' place, but Squirrel grew up on her parents' farm, and she didn't want to give it up, so we took over the place and made it our own.

Squirrel's sister Emma had had enough of country living and moved into town as soon as she could get out of the house. Eight years younger than Squirrel, she'd been a pest when I'd first known her. Squirrel called her Mudhen, said she was always getting into Squirrel's things, poking her beak in where she didn't belong. But all that was long ago.

Squirrel and I might be stuck in the past, but Emma was a "modern" woman. Just ask her. She'd wanted to get away from all that old country stuff. She took computer courses at the junior college and found her niche. She did consulting work these days. Right now she was working at the *Bay Herald*, digitizing all their old issues so subscribers could access them on the internet. Don't get me started on the internet. I remember when you could look at the old papers on microfilm for free. Now you had to buy the newspaper to get a look at the past issues.

Squirrel and her sister got along pretty well nowadays. The age difference had set them apart when they were younger, but they found that they had more in common as the years went by. Emma lived in town with her husband Frank and their two kids, Todd and Amy. Emma brought the kids out to the farm now and then, and Squirrel and I enjoyed showing them around. There was always something to do, and the kids always seemed to have a good time. Holiday dinners were usually at our place. The farm was a nice place to visit, but Emma was happier in town.

I turned into the lane that led to the house, crossing the little bridge that spanned the ditch beside the road. The runoff from the storm was filling the ditch and a blue heron was wading in the shallows. I drove between the fenced-in pastures on either side of the lane and parked behind the house.

There was a light on in the barn out back, and that meant Squirrel was out there tending to one chore or another. I'd see what she was up to later. I wanted to get out of my wet clothes. The heat in the car and the damp in my clothes had got me itching all over. I rushed up the steps to the back door and stopped in the mud room to hang up my wet jacket and hat.

The warmth of the kitchen felt good as I passed through on my way to our bedroom. Something smelled really good. I spotted the Dutch oven on the stove top, and stopped to lift the lid. Squirrel had been busy while I was poking around on the beach. Beef stew, one of my favorites. My stomach rumbled in anticipation. I headed to our bedroom to change clothes.

The upstairs bedrooms had been Squirrel's and Emma's when they were girls and still held a lot of their old things. A bookcase at the top of the stairs was filled with the books they'd collected growing up, including Emma's collection of Nancy Drew mysteries. The downstairs bedroom was for the old folks, which nowadays meant Squirrel and me.

We'd never had our own children to fill the upstairs rooms, which was a great sadness in our lives, especially for Squirrel. I'd been an only child and had learned to get along on my own, though I think I'd have been better off with a brother or sister to share things with.

When Emma got married and popped a couple of kids out right away, I knew Squirrel really envied her, but she put a good face on it and fussed over Emma's kids, pleased to be Auntie Sorrel. Emma allowed as how we could "borrow" her kids when we wanted to, and they did spend a lot of time with us when they were little.

Squirrel is smart—always was—and she found ways to keep the farm going and bring kids into our lives. When Emma's kids grew up and found lives of their own, she found other youngsters to take their place.

My mom had worked at the county library, and her love of books finally rubbed off on me when I went to college. I ended up teaching English at Bayside Junior High for thirty years before I retired. I'd spent a lot of time trying to spread Mom's gospel to other people's kids and had a lot of fun doing it. Kids that age are a challenge, but worth it—most of the time.

Squirrel and I kept the farm going all those years. She did most of the work, but I helped out. She loved the place and wanted to keep it running as long as she could. When it got to be too much for just the two of us, she found another way to keep her dream alive.

Squirrel turned the Posey place into a farm where people from town could come to see what a real farm was like "back in the day." Parents could bring their kids out to see where milk came from and could collect eggs still warm from the nest. They could pick apples and pumpkins in the fall, and take hayrides on the old flatbed trailer attached to the tractor.

Squirrel had been in the 4-H club at school and raised lambs to sell at the county fair. She'd stayed on as an adult volunteer, remembering the fun she'd had as a girl. Nowadays, kids from the city's 4-H club could pasture their calves and lambs at our place, fattening them up for the annual livestock sale at the fair.

I changed into dry clothes and put the wet things in the washer in the mud room. The storm had passed, leaving the yard "mud-luscious," and "puddle-wonderful," as e.e. cummings once said, so I slipped on a pair of rubber boots before heading out to the barn. The sun was heading for the horizon, painting the lingering clouds pink and red. I remembered Dad's "red skies at night, sailors' delight," thinking tomorrow might be a sunny spring day.

There was no sign of Squirrel when I entered the barn. Russell's old '53 Country Squire was under a tarp below the hayloft overhead. Squirrel didn't want to part with her dad's car. She thought maybe we'd have a son who'd want to fix it up. '53 was the fiftieth anniversary of the Ford Motor Company and the car had a special commemorative horn button. It also had the 239 cubic inch flathead V-8, the last year for that popular engine. But it was a station wagon, and not so popular with kids. Still, Squirrel wanted to keep it, so we put it up on blocks and covered it with a tarp. I'd rescued Mrs. Palmrose's old Chevy from her garage. Maybe someone would come along and give the Country Squire a new home.

Squirrel had set up a kind of classroom in the space

opposite the car, where the hayloft ended and the barn was open all the way to the roof. Photos of current and former 4-H members posed with their animals were hung on one wall. I'd cobbled up some benches for visitors to sit on with their children as Squirrel demonstrated one thing or another to our guests. I'd put up a chalkboard I'd rescued when they remodeled my school, a real slate slab they'd replaced with one of those abominable painted wooden things.

The barn had been electrified long ago, but there were only a couple of lights here and in the cow shed out back. I'd hung some more lights from the hay trolley suspended from the roof beam over the visitors' area. That gave Squirrel a chance to explain how the hay used to be hoisted into the barn through the door under the peak of the roof. Those lamps I'd added also threw enough light to show all the old farm tools we'd collected and hung from the walls.

What we called the cow shed was a little milking station added onto the back of the barn. When Squirrel's parents ran the place, they had a small dairy herd, five or six cows, and sold the milk to a dairy in town. We just had the one cow, a fawn-colored Guernsey we called Flossie. I looked in the doorway to see what Squirrel was up to.

She was sitting on the green three-legged milk stool, her head resting against Flossie's flank. Squirrel's hair had a lot of gray in it now, the red slowly fading, but it was a lovely color, like powdered cocoa. She'd put down a little tin of milk for Penny, the little banty hen that always showed up at milking time. Squirrel leaned against the cow, stroking her side, and watching as Penny dipped her beak in the milk and then tipped her head up to swallow. A few drops ran down onto her feathered breast.

Flossie had her head in the stanchion, placidly chewing on wisps of hay from the trough in front of her as Squirrel continued stroking her side. It was a lovely moment, so typical of Squirrel's fondness for animals. I knew Squirrel's gentle touch myself and, just for a second, wished I could trade places with Flossie.

I knocked on the doorframe, calling out, "Anybody home?

Squirrel looked my way and smiled. "Just us chickens," she said. It was an old joke between us. Flossie turned her head my way, gave me a sidelong glance, and went back to the trough, pulling hay into her mouth with her raspy tongue. Penny wiped her beak on the edge of the tin and pecked at a few grains of something on the floor.

Squirrel had already emptied the milk pail into the galvanized milk can. I made sure the lid was on tight and carried the can over to the fridge. She unlocked the stanchion for Flossie, and I shoveled out the cowflop while Squirrel washed down the floor.

"Did you find a good place to check out that metal detector?" she asked.

"I drove out to the south jetty, figured it was as good a place as any."

"You went all the way out there? Hardly anybody goes out there. I wouldn't think there'd be much to find."

"That's exactly why I went there. You know how I get sometimes. I just wanted to be by myself for a while."

Squirrel looked up at me then. There was a twinkle in her eye. "We went there once, didn't we? In that old Chevy you had."

Apparently she did remember. "That was another reason I went out there."

Squirrel put her arms around me. "Maybe we could go out there again sometime."

I knew she didn't mean it literally, but knowing she

thought we still could strike some sparks made me melt a little inside. "We could fix up the station wagon and go for a ride."

Squirrel took my arm and snuggled up against me as we walked back to the house.

We kicked off our boots, put on slippers, and went into the kitchen. Squirrel put on a pot of coffee, and I gathered things to set the table.

Squirrel scooped a couple of the dumplings on top of the stew and set them on our plates. She ladled the stew alongside the dumplings, and brought the steaming dishes to the table.

"This smells wonderful," I said. "I didn't get lunch, and I'm starving."

"It was kind of cold today. Made me think a pot of stew would be just the thing for dinner."

Squirrel filled two mugs with coffee and joined me at the kitchen table. "So what did you find with your super-duper metal detector? Anything good?"

I was attacking one of the fluffy dumplings, cutting it into smaller pieces and mixing it in with the stew. "Mostly just little things—old pop tops and a couple of coins. Walked all the way to the end of the spit and back." I managed to get in a forkful of stew before continuing. It was really good. "On the way back to the car, the detector went off again. I found something in the old streambed there."

I stirred another bit of dumpling into the stew, moving it around on the plate. "I'm not sure what it is, looks like a little metal box of some kind. It was raining pitchforks and hammer handles by then. I stuffed it in my pocket and made a dash for the car. I'm curious to see if there's anything inside, but this stew is too good to set aside. Let's take a look after dinner."

4

After dinner, I carried the dishes to the counter. Squirrel filled the sink, added some liquid detergent, and washed the dishes. The sun was down, and the light on the tankhouse cast its glow over the yard. I grabbed a tea towel and dried the dishes as Squirrel rinsed them and stacked them in the rack on the drainboard.

"The kids were here most of the day," Squirrel told me.

It was Saturday, always a busy day on the Posey farm. When school was out, the 4-H students spent most of the day tending to the calves and the lambs. The girls and the younger boys tended to raise lambs, but the older boys usually raised steers. By the time they were ready for the fair, those steers were pretty heavy and hard to handle.

"It's a good group this year. The kids, I mean. There was a little horseplay with the junior members," Squirrel said, smiling. "I don't know how you managed to teach that age group for so long."

"Junior high kids are a challenge, that's for sure. A lot of galloping hormones splashing about."

"Ted and his girlfriend were here all day. They're really good at keeping the younger ones in line. Both of them will be seniors next year. After they graduate, I don't know what we'll do without their help."

Teddy Mercer and Dolores Aguirre had both been students at Bayside my last year. They usually came out after school to feed the animals and look after things. They were a big help. The animals had to be fed every day, and most of the town kids couldn't get out here that often. Squirrel and I didn't mind taking up the slack, but having hard-working younger folk certainly made things easier.

I put away the dishes while Squirrel scrubbed the sink. "Maybe you can talk them into staying on as volunteers to help out after they graduate."

"Maybe—unless they're going away to college." Squirrel hung the dishrag over the rack to dry, looking out the window, though there was nothing to see. I knew she was thinking about the kids.

"Don't worry—it'll all work out. Teddy and Dolly were pretty pesty when they were junior high age. Look how they turned out."

She turned away from the sink. I'd hung up the dish towel and was going for a second cup of coffee. "So when are you going to show me what you found on the beach?"

I set my cup down on the table. "Now's as good a time as any," I said, heading to the mud room.

When I returned, Squirrel was wiping off the stove. She'd poured herself another cup, too. It was sitting on the table, the spoon standing in the cup, waiting to be stirred.

I held out the muddy box I'd found. "Here, take a look."

Squirrel took it carefully between her thumb and forefinger. "Yuck—let's clean it off first."

"It was buried in that muddy bank for a long time, looks like."

She put the box in the sink and ran water over it, scrubbing the dirt off with the little brush she kept beside the faucet. She frowned a little as the dirt came off, spreading over the bottom of the sink. "Probably should've tackled this first before I cleaned up. Oh, well."

I crowded next to her, trying to see what the thing was. When the dirt came off, Squirrel held it up so we could both see. It was a little box, about three inches wide and four inches long.

There was a design on the top. Squirrel got a paper towel and wiped away the rest of the dirt. The design had a lot of swirls and curlicues surrounding an open space in the middle with something written there. Rays fanned out on either side, extending to the ends and widening out to reach the corners.

"I thought it might be silver," I said. "But it's almost black."

Squirrel rubbed one of the raised swirls with her finger and held the box up to the light. It was shiny where she'd rubbed it. "I think you're right. It just needs to be polished." She opened the cupboard under the sink and moved the cleaners and things around till she found a jar of Wright's Silver Cream.

I wouldn't have gone to all that trouble, but Squirrel had clearly taken charge, and there was no stopping her when she set her mind on something She moistened the little sponge inside the jar and dipped it into the lavender paste. She spread the cream over the top of the box, scrubbing at the elaborate design. The sponge turned black as the tarnish came off. Squirrel rinsed the sponge several times, repeating the process until the only tarnish left remained in the deepest parts of the design.

I wanted to hold it myself and take a look, but Squirrel kept at it, polishing the edges and the bottom before she finally rinsed off the box and wiped it dry with the tea towel. Finally, she held it up to the light and turned it a little bit each way. "There's a name or something engraved in the center— those fancy letters that are hard to read."

"Let me see," I said, reaching into my pocket for my reading glasses. She handed it to me, and I turned it toward the light to get a better look. It was hard to make out what it said. The first letter looked like an O, with fancy swirls around it. The other letters were a little easier to figure out. "I think it says 'Olive.' " I handed her my reading glasses. "See what you think it says."

Squirrel put on the glasses and squinted at the writing. "I think you're right. 'Olive'—probably some girl's name." She shook the box and there was a little rattling sound. "I think there's something inside."

Squirrel ran her fingers around the edge, trying to open the box. "It's stuck pretty tight."

"Want me to try it?"

"No, you'll just ruin it, trying to force it open. Let me work on it a bit." She sat down at the table with the box in front of her. I retrieved my coffee cup and sat beside her, watching her as she tried to figure out how to get it open.

Squirrel pushed up along the edges of the lid with her long, graceful fingers. She'd always taken care of her hands. She wore gloves when she worked outdoors, and in spite of all the years of farm work, her strong hands were still soft and supple. She worked her way around the front and sides of the box, pushing up on the edges of the hinged lid until it finally popped open. She set the box down on the table and carefully raised the lid.

Apparently the box wasn't watertight. There was still some dirty water inside, but we hardly noticed. In the middle of the box, on some kind of cloth, maybe velvet, was a piece of jewelry on a tarnished silver chain.

"Wow," I said. "Look at that."

Squirrel carefully extricated it from the box, untangling it from the rotted cloth, and held it up. "Some kind of pendant on a chain. Let me clean it up so we can get a better look." She headed to the sink to wash it off.

I pulled out the cloth and wiped out the inside of the box. I took a closer look, turning the box over. There was something stamped on the bottom. I picked up my reading glasses from the end of the table where Squirrel had left them and put them on. I hate those things. My vision is just fine. I can see cars coming a mile down the road. But up close, everything is a blur. It can be really annoying sometimes.

I turned the box toward the light so I could see what was written on the bottom. It said "Vogel's." and there was a little outline of a bird next to the name.

Vogel's Jewelry had been in the same store downtown since the 1920s. There were other jewelry stores in town, but Vogel's was always the place for top of the line stuff. The store is on a corner, with windows along either side. Their window displays are famous. When I was a boy in the 1950s, they had these fabulous animated scenes in the windows at Christmas.

There was a "Honeymoon Rocket" that bobbed up and down with the happy couple on board as the moon rotated behind them. Another had half a dozen animated figures repairing and polishing a giant diamond solitaire ring. One of the workmen was sitting on the edge of the base, eating his lunch from the open lunch pail beside him. My favorite was an animated marching band with nine musicians that marched in unison, turning this way and that. A mirror behind them made it look like there were twice as many.

When I was nine or ten, I asked Mr. Vogel about those moving displays. He told me they were "Motion Machines," made by a company called Baranger that rented them out to jewelry stores to boost the stores' sales. I loved those displays. Not surprisingly, Vogel's was our first stop when Squirrel and I were looking to buy our wedding bands.

Squirrel brought the pendant back to the table, wiping it dry with a soft cloth.

"The box came from Vogel's." I said, showing her their trademark on the bottom.

She unfolded the cloth on the tabletop so I could see. "I don't know what it is, exactly. It's not like anything I've seen at Vogel's or any other jewelry store. It looks custom-made."

"Or maybe someone just used the Vogel's box to keep it in."

"Could be, but whatever the story is, it's something special." Squirrel held the pendant in her palm, the chain draped over the top of her hand. "The design is really unusual."

The pendant was about three inches from top to bottom and about an inch wide. Three black, triangular stones were mounted on a flat rectangle of what looked like polished bone or ivory. The stone triangles pointed downward, one above the other. They were wider at the flat top and shorter on the sides, the kind called isosceles.

"I've never seen anything like it either," I said. "What kind of stones d'ya think those are?"

"I don't know for certain, Billy. It might be onyx. You know I've never been much interested in jewelry."

That was for sure. I'd bought Squirrel bracelets and rings as anniversary gifts the first few years, but she never wore them much, just the wedding band. Saved me a lot of money over the years, but I always wished she'd let me buy her fancier things sometimes.

Squirrel turned the pendant over in her palm. "There's something on the back." She squinted at it, turning it one way and another. "What does it say?" She handed it to me.

I pushed my reading glasses up on my nose and took a look. The base on which the black stones were mounted was rounded on the corners and a warm ivory tone, almost like caramel. On the back it said "niwhdin." I had no idea what that meant. I grabbed a paper napkin from the holder in the middle of the table and carefully copied those letters. I had to look two or three times to be sure I got them right. Below that word, if that's what it was, was the letter J. The only other thing on the back was Vogel's trademark bird and the initials HV in one corner.

"I don't know what those letters mean," I told Squirrel, "but that's Vogel's trademark."

"I wonder whether they could tell us anything about it, if we took the pendant down to the store."

"I don't know. Who knows how long this thing was buried out there? Probably nobody down there would remember anything about it."

"Maybe not," Squirrel said. She put the pendant in the box and carefully tucked in the chain. She closed the lid gently and ran her finger over the design. "No harm in asking, though."

I could tell a trip to Vogel's was only a matter of time, but it would have to wait. I'd had enough for one day, and tomorrow was Sunday, a busy day on the Posey farm.

5

After breakfast, I washed my wet clothes from the day before and threw them in the dryer. That was another of the good things we had nowadays. I thought of all those Saturdays Mom spent washing clothes and lugging them outside to hang on the line. Having a dryer would have made her washdays a lot easier.

I stepped out on the back porch and surveyed the yard. It was a sunny spring morning, crisp and clear. A cold steam rose from the roof of the barn as the morning sun drew the moisture from the shingles. A little breeze caught the tail of the windmill, turning the blades to face the wind. A gasoline rainbow in one of the puddles reminded me of Mom's fanciful explanation that when lightning struck a rainbow, it broke it into pieces and scattered them on the ground.

The big oak tree beside the barn was beginning to get new leaves, and I could hear the steady tsip, tsip of the black phoebe perched on the wire fence at the edge of the pasture. I watched as he swooped out after a bug, circled back and landed on the fence post, scanning the yard for other victims.

It was mornings like this that made country living special, no matter what Squirrel's sister had to say about it. There were chores to be done for sure. Squirrel had already milked the cow. Teddy and Dolly and some of the others would show up later to tend to their animals. We could relax and enjoy the morning for another hour or two before they arrived.

Squirrel had just come in from the barn. She washed up at

the kitchen sink, poured herself a cup of coffee, and brought it over to join me at the table. "I talked to Emma yesterday," she said. She spooned some sugar into her cup and swirled it around, tapping the spoon against the side of the cup. "She said she and Frank might come out this afternoon. She asked if you'd tried out that metal detector yet."

That metal detector had actually been Emma's idea. She was full of ideas about getting us to "catch up with the times," as she put it. She'd given Squirrel a computer and gotten us hooked up with the internet. Emma'd shown her sister how "easy" it was to keep track of our finances on the farm. When Squirrel got the hang of it, she used the computer to create a record for each of the 4-H kids. She kept track of the animals' needs and monitored the students' attendance and their work with the livestock.

None of that stuff came easy to me, but Emma had roped me in, too. "You know how you like old stuff," she told me. "You ought to get one of those metal detectors. You might find some interesting things on one of your rambles."

Emma knew how I sometimes needed to get off by myself and give her sister a little peace. So when I stopped in at the sporting goods store to get a new fishing license, I found myself staring at a display of those metal detectors, and it didn't take long for the chatty salesman to reel me in.

"What did you tell her?"

"I just said you'd taken it with you to the beach yesterday. I figured you'd want to tell her yourself."

"Probably better that way—kind of make it a surprise." There was a lot of the old Mudhen in that girl. She still liked to poke her beak in other people's business, but nowadays it took the form of her efforts to be "helpful," signing us up with the internet, and all that "bringing us up to date" stuff. "Wait till they get here, then we can show them what I found."

Teddy and Dolly showed up around ten-thirty in his old International Scout, a '70s model his father'd had when he was Teddy's age. It was yellow and white, with the removable hardtop. I wasn't the only one who liked old stuff, it seemed.

When Squirrel and I went out to meet them, the two kids hopped out and strolled over to meet us. For some reason, they looked pretty pleased with themselves. I'd seen that look when they'd been students of mine. They were up to something, for sure.

"Good morning." Teddy said, grinning. "We stopped by the feed store, picked up those salt licks you ordered. They're in the back of the truck."

"Thanks for doing that," Squirrel said. "Saved me a trip to town."

"No problem, Mrs. Barnes." He looked like he was about to bust a gusset. "You tell her, Dolly."

"We got you something else, too," she said. "It's a surprise."

"Something to remember us by after we graduate," Teddy offered. "Come look in the truck." He took Dolly's hand and led the way.

Squirrel gave me a puzzled look. "What are those two up to?"

"Only one way to find out," I said, tipping my head toward the truck. "Let's take a look."

Squirrel put her arm in mine and we headed over to see what they'd brought. Dolly was sitting on the open tailgate, dangling her legs. Teddy stood beside her, still wearing that silly grin.

Dolly hopped down from the tailgate, moving closer to Teddy. "What do you think?" she said, pointing inside.

Two chickens stared back at us from inside a small

cage next to the salt licks. They were the strangest-looking chickens I'd ever seen. They had tufts of feathers sprouting from the sides of their heads and little bumpy combs on top. And no tailfeathers sticking up in back like all the other chickens!

Squirrel, though, knew right away what they were. "Araucanas," she said. "Wherever did you find them?"

"Mr. Olsen at the feed store ordered them for us. He found a breeder online who sold them."

"Of course, you know they lay blue eggs," Squirrel said. I knew that, too, but I'd never seen an Araucana chicken before.

"Yeah," Teddy said. "You can think of us every time you find a blue egg in the nest."

Squirrel smiled. "I sure will. But right now we need to build a pen to keep them isolated until the others get used to them. Our chickens won't like newcomers. They'll peck them to pieces if we introduce these two right away."

"The junior members can build a pen to keep them separate," Dolly offered. "Teddy and I can help them put it together."

"We just wanted to let you know how much we appreciate everything you've done for us," Teddy added.

"We'll work something out, I'm sure," Squirrel said. "Thank you so much. It was really nice of you. And I will think of you every time I find a blue egg in the nest."

I was pretty sure I was included in the "we" that would "work something out," but that was okay. I could tell Squirrel was pleased by the kids' thoughtfulness, even though it meant more work. But Teddy and Dolly were responsible kids who would follow through. Maybe their enthusiasm would inspire the junior members and keep them out of trouble.

Emma and Frank arrived in time for lunch, their new Land Rover splashing through the puddles in the driveway. I liked Frank, but I was pretty sure he wasn't the type for off-road adventures. Maybe a trip to the mountains to play in the snow, but Frank was an attorney and could afford better toys than most people. I was surprised that Emma let him get away with a gas guzzler like that. Twelve mpg in the city!

Some of the other 4-H kids arrived later in the morning, and Teddy and Dolly were out in the field, keeping an eye on things, making sure the kids were taking care of the animals and keeping the horseplay to a minimum.

Frank wore his usual dress slacks and a blue Oxford cloth shirt with a button-down collar. His Italian loafers weren't made for dodging puddles, and he carefully picked his way across the driveway to the back door. That was just Frank being himself. He seemed a little stuffy, but he was nice enough, and Emma and he seemed happy.

Emma had inherited her mom's dark hair and small stature, but she looked good in navy slacks and a white blouse with a colorful scarf. She wore fashionable boots that made her a little taller, though not nearly as tall as her husband.

We sat at the table after lunch, catching up on things. Frank, as usual, didn't have much to say. Emma and Squirrel did most of the talking when we got together. The sisters had grown a lot closer over the years. I usually just went with the flow, tossing in my two cents once in a while.

Emma eventually remembered what Squirrel had told her the day before, about my going to the beach to try out the metal detector. "Find anything interesting on your trip to the beach?" she asked, turning toward me.

"I did, actually. I didn't know what to expect at first, but I did find a few things. One of them was pretty interesting."

"Where'd you go? Sorrel just said you went to the beach."

"I went out to the south jetty."

Frank gave me a curious look. "Why'd you go out there? There's nothing to see. Hardly anyone ever goes out there."

"That was kind of the idea—get away from everybody, try out that thing without a bunch of people looking over my shoulder."

"Mom used to tell us stories about that place," Emma said. "There was something about a murder, or that beach being haunted. I don't remember exactly. She just said people weren't supposed to go there."

Squirrel patted Emma's arm. "You were little when Mom told us those stories." Emma looked annoyed, but Squirrel continued, "It supposedly happened just after the war. Mom said a couple was attacked when they were out there at night. The man was beaten up pretty bad, and the girl disappeared. I don't think anybody knows the whole story, but I remember our parents always telling us kids not to go out there."

Emma paused, thinking it over. "So what did you turn up on your trip to the 'haunted beach'?"

"Well, I found some little things, some old pop tops and a couple of coins, but when I was about to give up and head back to the car, I found something else. Wait a second, and I'll show you."

I went into the front room and retrieved the silver box from the mantel, where we'd left it the day before. I returned to the kitchen and set it on the table in front of Emma. "We're not sure what to make of it, but it looks like something really special. Open it up and take a look."

Emma picked up the box and turned it this way and that, looking at it carefully. Frank peered at it from across the table, trying to see for himself. "It says something on the top," he said. "It's hard to see without my reading glasses. Looks like 'Clive' maybe?"

"All those curlicues make it hard to read," Squirrel said. "But that first letter is an O. We're pretty sure it says 'Olive.' Go ahead and open it."

Emma popped open the top and raised the lid, peering inside. Her eyes widened when she saw the pendant. "Wow! I bet you were surprised when you saw this."

"The box was covered in mud and black with tarnish, but Squirrel cleaned it up."

Emma held up the pendant and looked at the design. She ran her fingertip over the black stones. "I've never seen anything like this before. Looks pretty fancy, though." She turned the pendant over. "There's something written on the back, too."

"The box has Vogel's trademark on the bottom," Squirrel said. "It's on the back of the pendant, too."

Frank held out his hand. "Can I see it, Emma?" He took a pair of reading glasses from his shirt pocket and put them on. He turned the pendant over in the palm of his hand, looking at both sides. "I see Vogel's trademark—that little bird. But what's that word in the middle? It just looks like a bunch of letters."

"We don't know what it means either," Squirrel said. "I thought maybe we could show it to someone at Vogel's and see what they could tell us."

"Maybe," Emma offered. "I don't know about the pendant, but the box looks pretty old, especially with that fancy design on the lid. Probably nobody at the store these days will know much about something this old."

"Might be worth a try," Frank said, handing the pendant back to Emma, who carefully placed it in the box.

Emma closed the lid and pushed the box into the center of the table. "Sure would be interesting to know more about it." She turned and looked at me. "So how do you like that new toy now?"

6

Vogel's Jewelry had occupied the same downtown corner at Third and E Sts. since the 1920s. The saloons and red light houses had been close to the docks in pioneer days, but a thriving business district had flourished just a few blocks away even then. Men with timber fortunes built multistory buildings, including a theater and an opera house, to show off their newly acquired wealth. Banks and office buildings with dime stores, restaurants, and department stores on the ground level lined the downtown streets leading away from the bay.

The rough joints were fading when Vogel's settled in at Third and E, but Two Street, as locals called Second, was still a pretty shady area, lined with bars and cheap hotels. Vogel's presence had done a lot to improve the area, and other stores had sprung up in the same block. The imposing façade of the Merchants' Bank across the street suggested character and stability, adding further assurance that the neighborhood was safe.

In the 1950s, as Buck's Landing grew and spread further south from the bay, a new shopping center on the other side of town had taken a toll on the downtown merchants. Some stores moved to the new mall. Other businesses closed, leaving a lot of empty storefronts downtown. Vogel's soldiered on, a steady presence that helped the remaining businesses weather the changing times.

In the '90s, the Downtown Merchants' Association came up with a plan to revive the area, creating an "Old Town" with a trendy atmosphere that appealed to locals and tourists alike. Pioneer buildings worth saving got facelifts. Others, too far gone to be saved, were razed and replaced with new "old style" buildings. Brick pavements and antique lampposts added charm to the streets.

Warehouses along the docks were torn down, replaced by three-story condominiums with balconies that looked out onto the bay. I missed the old places along the bayshore, like Hess' Emporium, where I once worked. Old man Hess sold architectural salvage items. He went out of business in the'50s when people wanted new things after the war. If he'd been around in the '90s, his business would have boomed as people dolled up the area.

All that was in my mind as Squirrel and I pulled up in front of Vogel's. The Merchants' Bank building across the street had stood vacant for years, but its classic design had saved it from demolition. It was now home to the Buck's Landing Heritage Society, a museum devoted to local history, with elaborate displays of stuffed birds, Indian artifacts, and items of local maritime history.

Vogel's looked the same as it always had, with five display windows on each side of the entrance on the corner of the building. Whether you walked along Third Street or came down E, you couldn't pass Vogel's without seeing what they had to offer. "Fine Jewelry since 1925" was spelled out in gold letters above the windows on both sides. An old-fashioned neon clock hanging over the corner entrance displayed the time to passersby in both directions.

A chime sounded as we entered the brightly-lit showroom with its rows of lighted display cases along the walls, each one filled with a collection of jewelry items that dazzled the eye.

An older woman, with a pair of reading glasses hanging from a lanyard around her neck, stepped out from behind the counter. "May I help you?" she said, smiling.

"Well, we hope so," I began. I knew the saleswoman was

anticipating making a sale and likely to be disappointed when she found out why we had come into the shop. I was beginning to think we were on a fool's mission, but I forged ahead. "We came across an old piece of jewelry from your shop, and we were wondering if you could tell us anything about it."

Squirrel set her purse on the counter and pulled out the silver box. "It's got your store's trademark on the bottom," she said, handing it to the woman. "I'm Sorrel Barnes, by the way. This is Billy, my husband."

"I'm Gladys Vogel," she said, shaking hands with both of us. She put on the reading glasses and turned the box over. "That's definitely our mark on the bottom." She carefully pried the lid open to look inside. When she saw the pendant, her eyes narrowed in doubt. "I've never seen anything like this in our store, though."

"Turn it over and look on the back," Squirrel said.

Gladys turned the pendant over, peering at what was written there. She didn't say anything for a minute or so as she studied the writing on the back of the pendant. "Well," she finally said, "it's definitely from our store. But it looks really old, especially the box. I don't recall anything like it during my time here."

I glanced at Squirrel, who was looking crestfallen. Her shoulders sagged a little, and I knew she shared my disappointment. We hadn't expected to learn much about the box and its contents, but we'd hoped to find out more than Gladys had to offer.

Gladys continued to stare at the pendant, turning it over in her hands. "Like I said, this is really old. Maybe my husband can tell you more. He's in the back, working on something. Let me ask him to come take a look at this." She laid the pendant next to the box on a velvet mat and walked to the back of the showroom.

Behind a glass partition, a man was seated at a worktable. Gladys went behind the partition, and the two spoke for a minute or so. The man rose and walked out with her to the front of the store.

"Hi, I'm Karl Vogel," he said, extending his hand to each of us in turn. Karl looked to be about our age. He had a magnifying visor pushed up on his forehead and sported a pair of glasses with small magnifying lenses at the corner that could be rotated into place. "Gladys says you've got something for us to look at."

"Yes," Squirrel said, "we'd appreciate anything you could tell us about a piece of jewelry we came across." We'd already decided to keep mum about where the pendant had come from until we knew more about it.

Karl Vogel peered at the writing on the lid of the box, turned it over, glanced at the familiar trademark, and set it back on the counter. He picked up the pendant, running his hand over the black stones. He turned it over and studied what was written there.

"Well, I don't recognize this piece, but I can tell you a little about it."

Squirrel leaned forward, resting her hands on the counter. "Anything you can tell us would be appreciated."

"My grandfather, Horst Vogel, made this." He pointed to the mark in the corner of the pendant. "HV—those are his initials. He always marked his work." He paused in thought, finally looking up at us.

"Grandpa was quite a guy. He was born in the old country in 1889, came over here in the twenties, started the business. People had money in those days, liked to spend it on nice stuff. The Depression put a damper on things, but he weathered that well enough till times got better.

He died in '61, but by then he had passed the business on to my dad."

"We bought our wedding bands here when we got married," I said, holding up my hand to show him.

"Probably bought those from my father. I grew up in the store, learned a lot from him, took over the store when he retired in the early '90s. He's gone now, but old folks still speak kindly of him."

"Anything else you can tell us about these things?" Squirrel asked.

"Well, the box is old, probably about the same age as the pendant. That Art Deco design was popular in Grandpa's day. I've seen a couple like it before. The pendant is a different story, though. I'd have to do some looking into the old records. Dad and Grandpa never threw anything away, got boxes of old papers in our storeroom. Nowadays, everything's on the computer."

He pulled out a cell phone from his pocket. "Let me take a picture so I can remember exactly what that pendant looks like. That design's got me wondering what Grandpa was up to. Maybe I can find something in his old files."

Karl snapped a couple of photos of the front and back of the pendant. "Get Gladys to take down your phone number, and I'll call you if I turn up anything. I'm not too busy today, maybe I can take a look this afternoon."

Squirrel and I thanked the Vogels profusely, gave them our cell phone numbers (another of Emma's attempts to bring us into the modern world), and left the store.

It was past lunchtime when we left Vogel's, and Squirrel suggested we head down to the boat basin and have lunch. We drove through the trendy Old Town area, headed toward the docks.

"Looks like they painted the old theater building,"

Squirrel said, pointing out the three-story structure.

"Yeah," I said. "It's nice they finally fixed it up. That red brick with the dark green trim really makes it stand out."

The building that housed the pioneer theater upstairs had seen a lot of early day stars, like P.T. Barnum and his troupe with General Tom Thumb, and even an appearance by the scandalous "Jersey Lily" Langtry. It had fallen into disrepair and sat idle for decades, but when the Indian casinos caught on and the local Native folks had new money, they bought the building and formed a partnership with the Merchants' Association. Together they restored the theater, and the Natives established a cultural center on the ground floor.

"It was just gray as long as I can remember," Squirrel said. "All the details were just painted out."

When the renovations were being planned, people were invited to come take a look in return for a donation, and Squirrel and I had marveled at the faded elegance of the old theater that had been hidden upstairs in the nondescript building.

"I remember when we got to look at the old theater. It was in bad shape. I'm glad somebody finally recognized all that history going to ruin upstairs. Seems like the Indians were the only ones interested in saving it and finally convinced the downtown merchants to step up."

"It was worth saving, for sure," Squirrel said as we drove on.

The waterfront had undergone a lot of changes, too. A newly-paved parking area allowed visitors easy access to a handsome boardwalk lined with food stalls and shops selling local crafts and souvenir items.

Squirrel led the way to Toli's Tacos, a favorite spot of hers. I knew she was looking forward to having Toli's "Fabulous Fish Tacos," but I missed getting one of Wally's Famous Footlongs from the old converted Airstream trailer on the street above, where the new townhouses looked out over the water. I wondered if the view from their balconies made up for the sour smell of the pulp mill across the bay.

After lunch, we got cones from Frozen in Time, a new shop that sold handcrafted treats from local dairies, and strolled along the boardwalk. At the end of the pier, we watched a couple of sailboats drifting out on the bay and leaned against the railing, looking out toward Mackey Island, once the scene of a massacre as white settlers drove out the last of the local Indians.

When the Indians were gone, lumber baron Noah Mackey built a mansion on the island so he could flaunt his wealth as he surveyed his empire on the shore of Heron Bay. Supposedly he fell on hard times, and the extravagant Victorian monstrosity was left to ruin.

Efforts by tribal groups in recent years had forced the city to cede the island back to the Indians, and plans were being made for a permanent memorial on the island, with historical exhibits housed in a small museum. When it was completed, charter boat tours of the bay would include a stop at the island.

Squirrel's cell phone rang. She handed me her cone and fumbled in her purse.

"Hello?" She looked at me then. "It's Mr. Vogel." She punched the speaker button on her phone. I recognized Karl Vogel's voice.

"I just wanted to let you folks know I found something in my grandfather's files. You might want to stop by and take a look."

Squirrel threw a questioning look my way. I nodded in agreement. "We'd be glad to. We're at the boat basin. We'll come over in a few minutes if that's okay."

"I'll be here." There was a pause before he ended the call, saying, "You might want to brush up on your German on the way over."

7

We found a parking space in front of the museum and crossed the street to Vogel's, eager to learn what Karl Vogel had discovered.

The chime over the door sounded as we entered the shop. Gladys looked up from the counter where she was arranging rings in a velvet tray.

"Oh, hi," she said. "Karl told me you were coming back. I'll let him know you're here."

She headed toward the back, but Karl was already coming out from behind the glass partition, pushing that magnifying visor up on his forehead. He waved some papers in his hand as he crossed the floor. "I'm glad you came back. I wanted to show you what I found." He laid the papers on the counter where we stood.

"Like I said, Grandpa and Dad never threw anything out. It took me a while, but they were pretty organized. I was going through the files, based on my best guess about the age of that silver box."

Squirrel was listening intently to what Karl said. So was I, but I couldn't take my eyes off those papers on the counter. I wanted to know what Karl had found.

"It was old enough to be before my dad's time, so I started going through Grandpa's files. Unfortunately, all his records are in German, but this one caught my eye."

He held up a yellowed invoice. "See, at the top? It says 'Sonderbestellung.' That's 'special order,' I think. Dad was better at German than I am. Besides, Grandpa's old German script is pretty hard to read. Anyway, there were a number of these special order invoices."

Karl pointed to another phrase. "This is what made me think I'd found the right one." Squirrel and 1 peered at the spot where he was pointing. He was right about the script. I had no idea what it said.

" 'Kundindesign mit Onyx und Elchhorn.' That Onyx und Elchhorn part caught my attention. Those black stones are onyx, for sure. I thought that base might be ivory at first, but the color and grain aren't quite right. If it's elk horn, that would explain the difference."

"What's that other word?" Squirrel asked, "that Kundin-part?"

"Well, I think that means 'customer,' like maybe the person who ordered the pendant brought in his own design. There's no name on the order form, which seems a little odd, but Grandpa had his own way of doing things. Maybe the customer was somebody he knew."

I looked at the invoice again. "Are you sure this is the same pendant?" Maybe your grandfather made others like it."

Karl looked up from the invoice. "I was thinking the same thing, but here's what convinced me I'd found the original order." He folded back the top sheet to reveal another paper stapled behind. It was just a plain white sheet, yellowed around the edges, with some foxing from age. But there on the page was a pencil drawing of a pendant that was a dead ringer for the one we'd found.

Squirrel let out a little gasp when she saw the drawing. "That's it! It's just like the pendant in the box."

"Here's the clincher," Karl said, pointing to some words near the bottom of the page. "It says 'Inschrift,' which means inscription. I don't know what the word below that means. That n-i-w-h-d-i-n," he said, spelling it out. "That's not a German word—must be something the customer wanted.

Could mean anything. The J below that is probably an initial, maybe the customer's."

Squirrel ran her finger over the drawing, a puzzled look on her face. "Well, you've certainly been helpful," she said, looking up at Karl Vogel.

I couldn't help myself. "Any idea how much that pendant is worth?"

"According to this," Karl said, pointing to the bottom of the order form, "it cost forty-nine dollars in 1945. It's probably worth six or seven hundred today. Maybe more if you add in the value of the box." He smiled, looking at each of us in turn. "You interested in selling it?"

Squirrel spoke up. "I'm not much for wearing jewelry, but I think we'd like to keep it, at least for a while." She looked at me for confirmation.

"We'd like to find out more about it if we can," I said. "Thanks for looking into this for us."

"I'm glad to help. I was curious about the pendant as soon as I saw it. The papers I found explain a little, but they don't really tell us much."

He folded the invoice back over the drawing and glanced at it. "There is one more thing, though. The original order is dated at the top. See here," he said, pointing to a line partially hidden where the pages were stapled together. It was marked "22.6.46."

"That's June 22," Karl said. "Maybe it was one of those June wedding gifts."

"Could have been, I suppose," Squirrel said. "Whatever it all means, we're grateful for your help. Thanks for going to all that trouble for us."

"I didn't mind at all. As I said, you piqued my curiosity. When I saw my grandfather's mark, I wanted to see what I could find out about that piece."

I added my thanks, and Squirrel and I left the shop. We crossed the street and got in the car. As we settled in, fastening our seatbelts, Squirrel said, "Well, we found out a lot, but at the same time, we didn't really find out anything."

"Yeah," I said. "We know a little bit more about the jewelry. Too bad we don't know anything more about the people—Olive and whoever J was."

"And that strange word on the back."

"That, too," I said, starting the car.

We'd learned quite a bit from Karl Vogel, but he'd really only confirmed what we already knew: the box and the pendant came from Vogel's. The trademarks had told us that much. The revelations about his grandfather added something, but didn't tell us any more about the mysterious word on the back or the name Olive on the lid of the box.

Squirrel phoned her sister while I drove us back home. I thought it could wait, but Squirrel was eager to tell Emma what we'd found out at Vogel's. Emma agreed that what we learned still left us pretty much in the dark about the pendant, even though the new details were interesting.

It was late in the afternoon when we got home. Squirrel and I changed out of our street clothes, put on our work jackets and boots, and walked out to the barn. Flossie was waiting in the field. She looked up when she saw us coming, moving toward the gate outside the cow shed. Squirrel opened the gate to let her in, and I headed into the barn to see if I could find some material to build a pen for the new chickens.

Squirrel had sketched some designs on paper, so I had a good idea what she wanted. Nothing much gets thrown away on a farm, and the barn usually yields something useful if you're looking for stuff for a new project.

When Squirrel's father saw me getting ready to go into town to get something one time, he told me, "Don't be runnin' into town every time you come up short doin' something. There's always stuff lyin' around here you can use. Learn to improvise, son."

Improvise was Russ's watchword. I'd heard him say it time and again. At first I thought he was just being cheap. But he was usually right. Most of the time we could do with what we had. We had lots of "stuff" in the barn or one of the outbuildings: barbed wire, baling twine, chicken wire, fence posts, wood that was too good to throw away or burn. The shelves below the workbench held jars and coffee cans filled with nuts and bolts of every kind. Tools of every description hung from the wall above.

I'd worked in the hardware store with my dad when I was a kid. My first thought when I "came up short" on a project was to run to Ace or True Value to get what I needed. But I'd come around to Russ's way of thinking. Nowadays the hardware store in town was usually a last resort.

Russell Posey was clever with all his improvising. Even worn out things got repurposed sometimes. One of my favorites was the automatic closer for the gate that let Flossie in from the pasture. He'd fashioned it from a length of chain and an old cast iron window sash weight. When I opened the gate to let Flossie into the barn, the weight dangling from the chain pulled the gate shut behind me—simple but clever.

Our interest in the mysterious pendant simmered on the back burner as we got caught up in more immediate concerns, notably what to do with those Araucanas to keep them safe while the other chickens got used to having them around.

I scrounged up some metal fence posts and Teddy and I

fenced off a corner of the chicken yard. I risked life and limb holding the posts while Teddy wielded the maul and drove them into the rain-softened ground. Some used chicken wire fastened to the lugs on the metal posts gave the new birds a corner of the yard where they would be safe.

Under a tarp behind the chicken house I found Emma's old rabbit hutch, the one she'd used when she entered her California Whites in the county fair. It had a sturdy wooden frame and a tarpaper roof, with wire covering the sides and the front. There was a hinged door in front, too. It was just the right size for a pair of chickens.

Wooden legs under the hutch kept it off the ground, which was perfect for the birds. A couple of nesting boxes and a little ramp so they could go in and out was all we needed. Those would be good projects to keep the junior members busy.

During the week, I got Teddy to help me move the old hutch over closer to the chicken yard. It was too heavy to carry, so we laid it on the tarp and dragged it over. Teddy gave me a funny look when I suggested moving the hutch that way. I knew he was thinking we could just carry it over if one of us wasn't so old, but he didn't say anything. He was a nice kid.

"Work smart," Squirrel's dad told me. "Better than workin' hard. Think about what needs doin'. There's always an easier way." It was another pearl of wisdom from Russell Posey.

Teddy and I stood the hutch up and looked it over. "It looks pretty good," he said.

The tarp had protected it pretty well, but it was still dirty, covered with years of accumulated grime. "Let's wash it off, see what's under all that dirt." We headed over to the faucet at the corner of the chicken yard. Teddy grabbed the end of the hose and dragged it over to the rabbit cage. When he gave me the thumbs up, I turned on the faucet and he hosed it down. He took his time, stopping now and then to pluck at the spider webs that were stuck in the corners and hard to dislodge.

When he was done, I turned off the water and we took another look. "Looks a lot better," I said, thanking Teddy.

He picked at a strip of peeling paint. "It'd be even better with a coat of paint. Maybe I can get the little kids to do that when they come out next time."

"Sounds good to me."

On Saturday morning, the kids arrived to tend their animals. I think they were as happy to see each other as they were to see their lambs and calves. They headed out to the fields to feed the animals, clean up the sheds where they sheltered, and make sure the troughs were filled with clean water. Teddy and Dolly helped them put out the new salt licks and check their charges for any signs of health problems. They also made sure the kids wrote everything down in their record books, keeping track of feed costs, time spent, and everything related to their projects. Squirrel would check these from time to time, keeping her own notes on each youngster's progress.

Squirrel and some of the parents put together a lunch for the kids when the work was done. Afterward, Dolly and Teddy rounded up a couple of the junior members and got them to volunteer to finish refurbishing the Araucanas' new home.

Bobby Cantwell, who had an obvious crush on Dolly, didn't need to be talked into doing anything she wanted. He'd had his hand raised before she was even finished explaining what needed to be done. Carla Spencer wasn't quite so eager, but she'd seen those funny-looking chickens and wanted to spend more time getting to know them.

Teddy took the door off the hutch so the new pullets could go in and out, and Dolly got Bobby to nail some wooden cleats to the plank that would serve as a ramp between the hutch and the ground. He bent over a few nails in his haste to please Dolly, but she showed him how to take his time and hammer them in correctly. He beamed as she fussed over him.

Teddy got Carla set up with a paint can and a brush, and she started in on the hutch. When Bobby finished with the ramp, Teddy found another brush for Bobby to help with the painting.

Squirrel and I were cleaning up after lunch as the parents gathered up things, preparing to leave. Teddy and Dolly came over to say goodbye, leaving Bobby and Carla to finish painting the hutch. Leaving them alone was not a good idea.

It didn't take long for the shouting to start. It was one of those "Are, too!"—"Am not!" arguments that kids that age are so fond of. I remembered them well from my days teaching junior high.

By the time Squirrel and I reached the chicken yard, Bobby was waving his paintbrush in Carla's face, looking like he was about to smack her with it. Carla had the bail of the paint can in one hand, her other hand on the bottom, most likely getting ready to shower Bobby with white paint.

After first making them put down their "weapons," we managed to calm them down and negotiate a truce. Apparently Bobby didn't like the way Carla was doing the painting, pointing out some places where the paint had run, and told her she was "doing it all wrong." This was the same boy who couldn't pound in a nail without bending it over just a little while ago. My sympathies lay with Carla, who was undoubtedly doing the best she could. Perfection was hardly the goal here.

Teddy and Dolly returned to supervise, and with a few frowns and scowls, the kids finished up the painting. The refurbished hutch looked good, a perfect home for the Araucanas as they settled in.

Squirrel and I were reviewing the day's events after dinner. We were sitting at the kitchen table, chuckling over the squabble between Bobby and Carla, when the phone rang. Squirrel pushed back her chair and crossed the kitchen to the wall phone.

"Hello… Oh, hi Emma, how are you?"

There was a pause as Squirrel listened to her sister. Those two had come a long way together. Emma'd gotten us those cell phones, but she knew her sister well enough to call the house phone first, figuring Squirrel wasn't walking around the house with that thing in her pocket.

These days, Squirrel only called Emma "Mudhen" if she was mad at her, and usually not to her face. And I was the only one who called Sorrel by her nickname.

Squirrel looked my way as she listened to her sister. She nodded, as if Emma could see, saying, "I guess so. Sure." There was another long pause. "All right, then. We'll see you on Monday."

She hung up the receiver, giving me a puzzled look. "Emma wants us to come to her office at the *Herald* on Monday. She says she found something in the archives we need to see."

8

Emma's call Saturday night had aroused our curiosity, and we'd speculated during the day on Sunday about what she could have found that was so important she couldn't have just told us about it on the phone. But Emma did things her own way, and so we headed to town on Monday morning to see what she had to show us.

The *Bay Herald* had been serving up the local news since the 1850s, founded only a few years after Buck's Landing itself. Originally located in the heart of downtown, the newspaper had moved its offices to Sixth and J Streets during the revitalization of the business district. Other businesses had followed suit, moving further south from the bay as the town grew.

The jail next to the courthouse was now a three-story monstrosity. An old mansard-roofed house next door, built in the 1870s, had been razed to provide parking for the courthouse and the jail. Some buildings escaped the bulldozer and were repurposed and given new life.

The *Herald* was still close to downtown, housed in a new building built for the purpose on a half-block lot on Sixth Street when another of the pioneer homes was demolished. A stately Victorian across the street had been dolled up with a three-color paint job and reborn as a law office, the sign for *Randall and Trent, Attorneys at Law* prominently displayed beside the century-old palm tree out front.

The *Herald*'s modern three-story building looked as out of place among the older buildings as a ballerina at a sock hop. The architects hadn't worried about trying to fit into the neighborhood. The concrete and glass exterior would be there long after the relics from the past were gone.

One of those relics occupied the other half of the block, a stately home built long ago with timber money. A wrought iron fence separated the house from the street, and a pair of giant palm trees, that typical bit of Victorian whimsy, flanked the entrance to the house. An alley separated the mansion from the newspaper office, leading both to the carriage house and the loading dock at the rear of the *Herald* building.

Side by side, the two buildings told their separate stories. Founded in the past, the *Herald* kept up with the changing times, reporting on the latest news. The old house told another story, a monument to times past and former glories and people fading in memory. The newspaper reported what went on in town, but people gossiped about what went on in the old place next door.

I'd heard the stories myself. Supposedly an old lady lived there with a motley collection of cats. There was a gallery on the second floor that overlooked the main floor, and people said she'd had "catwalks" built that crossed from one side of the gallery to the other so the cats could roam around to their hearts' delight. That sounded pretty far-fetched to me, but people say outrageous things sometimes, especially when they don't know the real story.

Squirrel and I pulled up in front of the newspaper office, parking on the street. A directory at the entrance listed a number of offices located on the first floor, rented out to an accounting firm and a couple of community affairs organizations. The *Herald*'s main office was just inside the front door.

A receptionist with a telephone headset was stationed at her desk behind the counter when we walked in. She was staring at her computer screen as she typed, frowning once or twice before she stopped typing to look up at us.

"Good morning," she said, smiling. "How can I help you?"

"We're here to see my sister Emma," Squirrel said. "Emma Posey—she's working on digitizing the paper's old issues."

Emma, ever the modern woman, hadn't taken her husband's name when they got married. "Emma Simmons," she'd declared, "too many m's." And she wasn't about to be "hyphenated," either. I was glad Squirrel had gone with tradition. She kept the Posey name on the farm, which was special to her, but she was Sorrel Barnes, and that was special to me.

"The archives are upstairs on the third floor. Halfway down on the left when you get out of the elevator. I'll call up and let her know you're coming."

We thanked her and headed down the hall to the elevator. Framed issues on the walls displayed the *Herald's* featured stories from past years. A sharp-eyed fellow with mutton chop whiskers stared at us from a portrait alongside the elevator doors. The brass plate at the bottom of the frame identified him as Horace Huddleson, "Our Founder."

Emma's office was a crowded space with racks of microfilm reels and more framed prints of old issues from the newspaper archives. When we entered, Emma was at her desk, seated behind an impressive array of equipment. Peering over her reading glasses, she looked up and smiled. "Oh, hi. I'm glad you're here. I've got something to show you."

That was Emma, not big on formalities. She got down to business right away. I wondered if we were taking her away from her work, but I needn't have worried. When Squirrel asked about all the equipment, Emma beamed, delighted to give us a tour of her digital empire.

"This is my FlexScan machine," she said, indicating a black box with a microfilm reel on each side and what looked like a tall camera lens standing in the middle between the reels.

"The film has to be carefully threaded on the machine. Then," pointing to the computer monitor beside the FlexScan gizmo, "I adjust the settings on the computer for the film width and determine the reduction ratio, which is pretty tricky."

I got lost when Emma began to explain how the reduction ratio was important in determining the "true DPI of the image," but it was obvious Emma was proud of what she did, and I listened politely as she continued to explain the digitizing process. A glance at Squirrel told me she was just as lost as I was, but she struggled to follow along, asking a question now and then.

Emma talked us through the adjustments for focus, lighting, and exposure. "Then it's time to scan," she said excitedly. She showed us some examples on the screen, explaining how she monitors the images as they scroll by, making manual adjustments from time to time.

"Well," she said, looking up at us, "that's probably more than you wanted to hear. Sorry—I get carried away sometimes. Let me find what I wanted to show you."

She walked to a table against the opposite wall, rummaged among some papers on top, and returned with several photocopied sheets. "These are from some issues I've been working on. I figured you'd want something you could hold in your hand, so I made copies for you.

"I'm going through the 1940s now, and I came across this article." Emma passed the top sheet of paper to Squirrel. I leaned over to get a look at what she'd found. It was the front page from the *Herald*'s issue of Monday, July 1st, 1946. The headline declared: "Mill Workers Strike over Working Conditions."

I didn't understand why Emma'd found this page so interesting till I noticed she'd circled a small article in the bottom left corner. The whole page had been reduced to fit on a single sheet, and the grainy image was hard to read. I could just make out the heading, "Unidentified Man Found Beaten on South Jetty Beach."

"I think this is the story that Mom told us about," Emma said. "It's hard to read, so I made a copy of the article and enlarged it." Here—take a look," she said, handing us another of the printed sheets.

The article was small, only a few column inches, and didn't offer a lot of information, other than a brief summary of events. "Sheriff's deputies called to the south jetty of Heron Bay in the early hours found an unconscious male in his car. The man appeared to be the victim of a savage beating, his face bloodied and his clothes torn." The article went on to say the discovery had been made by a local man who'd arrived at the beach before daylight, hoping to take advantage of the low tide at that hour and dig for clams. The unidentified victim was taken to Bay General, and the investigation was ongoing.

Squirrel looked at Emma. "Well, this could be what caused all those tales about the south jetty, but the article doesn't really tell us much about what happened out there."

Emma handed Squirrel another page. "There were other articles. Here's another story from the following day."

The article was a follow-up to the previous day's story, with a few added details. It was apparently noteworthy enough to make the front page, but still below the fold. A melee erupting with the striking mill workers had top billing.

"Witness Describes Grisly Discovery on South Jetty Beach," the article declared. The clam digger who'd found the man, a fellow named Philo Granstaff, had been interviewed by a reporter. "It was still pretty dark when I got to the beach, but I saw the car door was open. The man's legs were sticking out, so I decided to take a look. That fella was slumped over on the seat. He was kinda dark-complected. I thought he was just some drunk Indian passed out in his car—till I saw the blood."

The article went on to say that the victim hadn't regained consciousness and was still in the hospital. Sheriff's deputies were still waiting to interview him.

"There wasn't anything more for a couple of days," Emma said. "Then I found this in the Fourth of July issue. The front page was taken up with the plans for celebrating the holiday, so it got pushed back to page six. Take a look," she said, handing Squirrel another page.

The article was titled, "Victim of South Jetty Beating Identified." I leaned closer to read along. "Sheriff's deputies have identified the man found Monday as Jacob 'Jake' Whitehorse, a recently-returned veteran of the war in Europe. Regaining consciousness after three days at Bay General, the victim claimed he was assaulted by three men while parked at the beach with a woman friend. Whitehorse claimed he didn't know his assailants, and refused to identify the woman, whose identity is still unknown. Authorities are continuing to investigate the incident."

"There wasn't any more after that," Emma said, shrugging her shoulders. "Makes me wonder what really happened out there."

I looked at Squirrel. She pursed her lips in thought for a moment. "Sounds like nobody knows for sure—probably explains all the stories parents told their children when we were growing up."

"This Jake guy tells the cops he doesn't know who beat him up?" I said. "Sounds odd to me. And what about the mysterious 'woman friend'? Why wouldn't he say who he was with? There's more to that story."

"He was probably just trying to protect her," Emma said. "You know, keep her name out of the papers."

"Maybe they were in love," Squirrel offered.

"Could be," Emma said. "I tried to find out more, but I couldn't come up with anything,. He's not in the phone book, but then he'd be pretty old if he's still alive. I looked through the *Herald's* obits, but didn't find anything there, either."

Squirrel glanced at the photocopies again, then looked up at her sister. "Maybe he just moved away."

"I suppose," Emma said. "But I'm not convinced that's all there is to the story." She picked up the pages, tapped them on the desk into a neat stack, and looked my way. "Your poking around out there on the south jetty's got my antenna up. I'll keep looking, let you know if I find anything more."

Squirrel and I stayed a while longer to chat with Emma. She really enjoyed working at the *Herald* and gave us the nickel tour of the plant before we left. I liked the press room especially, where the whirling machines were cranking out the evening edition. It made me wish I could take my junior high students there on a field trip—almost.

On the way home, we talked about what Emma'd found in the paper's archives.

"The articles Emma found were pretty interesting," I said, "but disappointing, too. "It sheds a little light on those stories we heard when we were kids, but I don't know that it means much."

"Emma's always liked mysteries. She's still got all those Nancy Drews in the bookcase upstairs."

Squirrel and Emma hadn't always gotten along when they were kids. They weren't exactly "two peas in a pod", as people like to say. Emma was small and dark-haired like her Mother. Squirrel'd taken after their red-haired father. She called her little sister "Mudhen" back then, said she was always poking her beak into Squirrel's room and getting into things. The difference in their ages didn't matter much these days, but Emma hadn't lost that curious nature.

I slowed as we neared our driveway, signaling my intention to turn. "She seemed to think there might be some connection between what went on out there after the war and that box I found. Seems like quite a stretch, if you ask me."

Squirrel looked at me, tilting her head and raising an eyebrow, "Like you said, Billy, there's more to the story."

9

The first thing I noticed when we turned into the driveway was Teddy's International Scout parked near the barn. He didn't usually come out on Mondays, but it was after school hours, so it wasn't a total surprise. He was raising a Charolais steer, a big white beast that promised to be a handful when it was grown. It already weighed over five hundred pounds.

At the fair Teddy would be judged on how he and his steer worked together. He'd be judged on how well the animal would lead for him and how well it would stand for him with its feet in the right place. Teddy had spent a lot of time getting "Charlie" to wear a halter and let Teddy lead him around the pasture.

Teddy used a special stick with a hook on the end to teach the steer to "place" his feet. Every time the steer stopped, his feet needed to be straight, the front feet next to each other and the same with the back feet. The hook was just the right size to fit around the steer's lower leg and move his hoof into the right place. Teddy also used the stick to rub Charlie's chest and belly, which helped the animal relax. The two of them were making progress, but Charlie wasn't always in a cooperative mood, and it was slow going at times.

As we pulled up to the house, I noticed Dolly sitting on the Scout's tailgate. Teddy was hovering over her, and I knew something was wrong. I drove over to the barn to see what was up. Squirrel and I got out of the car and rushed over to see what had happened.

Dolly's right boot was lying on its side on the tailgate, and Teddy was holding her foot in his hands. She looked like she'd been crying.

"What happened?" Squirrel asked, looking first at Dolly, then at Teddy.

Teddy turned to look at Squirrel. "I was leading Charlie around, showing Dolly how good he was getting. I was trying to place his front feet when he stepped sideways—"

"And stomped on my foot! "Dolly said. "I was coming along behind them, and that damned steer decided to back up. Look at my foot!"

Squirrel gently took hold of Dolly's foot, examining it carefully. There was a bruise on the instep and her toes were turning purple.

"Ow, that hurts!" Dolly wiped her nose on the sleeve of her jacket.

Squirrel continued her examination. "It looks like something might be broken. We better get some ice on that foot. Drive her up to the house, Teddy. We'll get some ice from the fridge."

Squirrel went to get the ice. With Dolly still sitting on the tailgate, Teddy turned his truck around and drove slowly back to the house while I followed along behind them.

Squirrel came outside a couple of minutes later, with a bag of ice wrapped in a towel. I could tell how worried Teddy was when he lifted Dolly from the tailgate and carried her over to a lawn chair beside the porch. I got a wooden box from the porch and Teddy propped Dolly's foot up. Dolly flinched when Squirrel applied the ice pack, but Squirrel fussed over her, telling her to sit back in the chair. "Leave it on for a while. It'll help with the swelling."

Emma's revelations about the incident at the beach disappeared as I thought about Dolly's injury. The 4-H kids needed supervision, and their parents and one or both of us were always here when the kids were around. But Teddy and Dolly were seniors, and we usually didn't worry much about watching out for them. They should have let us know they were coming, though this probably would have happened anyway.

What to do now? That was the question. We had to call Dolly's parents, for sure. We couldn't just let Teddy drop her off at home, hoping everything would be fine. Squirrel and I were responsible for what happened at our place.

"We'd better call your parents," I said. Dolly frowned at me, her shoulders drooping. She looked like she felt guilty.

Squirrel looked up from tending to Dolly's foot and smiled. "Don't worry. I'll talk to your mom. It'll be okay."

Dolly adored her father. Dr. Aguirre was a large animal vet, who had treated Flossie a couple of times. Dolly'd inherited his love of creatures great and small. She helped her dad out in his practice and sometimes accompanied him on his farm visits. With Teddy already a 4-H member, it didn't take much persuasion to get Dolly to join.

Dolly's father seemed like a solid guy to me. I thought Dolly was acting like she'd done something wrong, that somehow her father would be disappointed that she'd let that steer step on her foot. I didn't think she had anything to worry about. I bet her father'd had his foot tromped on more than once. Her mother was a different story.

I'd only spoken to Lorna Aguirre a couple of times. She was nice enough, but it always seemed to me she fussed over her daughter more than was necessary. Dolly was a young woman now, no longer Mama's little girl who played in the sandbox and held tea parties with imaginary friends. Her mom needed to let Dolly spread her wings a little bit.

Squirrel thought Dolly would be more comfortable riding in our car instead of bouncing around in Teddy's truck. The two of them helped Dolly into the car and they headed into town with Teddy following in the Scout. I watched till they were out of sight and headed to the cow shed to deal with Flossie.

I forked some hay into the feed trough and scooped up some barley and oats to spread on top. Flossie was waiting at the gate. I let her into the shed and locked her head in the stanchion. As I dragged over the milking stool and pail, she gave me a baleful look, a wisp of hay hanging from her mouth.

I glanced at the cow kickers hanging on the wall. When I first tried milking Flossie, she'd fussed and kicked up a storm, knocking over the pail and smacking me in the shin. Those hobbles had come in handy then. But Flossie and I had reached a shaky détente over the years. It was obvious she preferred Squirrel's gentle touch to my ham-fisted efforts, but nowadays she put up with me with only the occasional dirty look. When I got a rhythm going, she let down her milk and munched away contentedly.

I leaned against Flossie's flank, the steady shush shush of the milk hitting the pail lulling me into thinking about the day's events. Squirrel would see that Dolly got home all right and do her best to calm Lorna's fears and keep her from taking things out on Teddy. I'd get all the details when Squirrel got back.

After mulling that over for a while, I thought about our trip to town to see Emma and what she'd discovered in the *Herald's* archives. It seemed strange that Emma hadn't found any other articles about the incident on the beach after the few she'd shown us. A man had been beaten half to death out there, but there wasn't any follow up in the press? The sheriff should have been beating the bushes to find out what went on and round up some suspects, but the story just seemed to have stalled somehow. It made me wonder what else Emma might find in the archives.

It was getting dark when I finished the milking and let Flossie out into the pasture. Squirrel had been gone a long time. I was heading back to the house when she pulled into the driveway. I walked over to find out how it went with Dolly's mom.

"You know what a fussbudget Lorna is," Squirrel said. "She gave Teddy a look that stopped him in his tracks when he tried to explain what happened. I felt sorry for him. It wasn't like he did anything wrong."

"That steer is a handful. I'm surprised he hasn't mashed Teddy's foot."

"Yeah, me too. Her husband's a vet. She should know by now that stuff like this happens all the time."

"I'm sure she does know," I said. "They just aren't supposed to happen to her daughter."

"You're right about that. Anyway, she calmed down after a while, but she wanted to have Dolly checked out. Her husband was out on a call, so we sent Teddy home and I drove them to the emergency room.

"They x-rayed her foot. It turns out she has a hairline fracture. They sent her home with crutches and one of those walking boot things. She has to stay off her foot for a week. After that she can get by with the walking boot if she's careful."

"Dolly looked guilty," I said. "Kind of like she thought she was in trouble somehow. I wondered if she was worried about what her dad would say."

"I noticed that look, too. Dolly didn't say much in the car on the way to town. I thought maybe it was just because her foot hurt so bad." Squirrel looked at me and smiled. "It turned out she was worried about missing out on the prom."

I should have known there was more going on in Dolly's mind than the pain in her foot. Old as I am, the feminine mind is still a mystery. "It's only April," I managed. "She should be fine by prom time."

"That's what I told her. She still looked worried, but she seemed to calm down a little. The doctor gave her some painkillers and sent her home. Her mom and I helped her with the crutches and got her into the house and situated on the couch. When I left, she was already on the phone, talking to Teddy."

"Sounds like she's going to be fine."

"As long as she 'steers' clear of Charlie," Squirrel said, raising an eyebrow.

10

So far, Emma's dive into the *Herald's* archives hadn't turned up anything new. She was busy digitizing issues from the '50s now, but she claimed she was still looking into the incident on the beach, determined to learn more about that Whitehorse fellow and what went on out there. April turned into May without any further revelations from Emma. Warm sunny days pushed the memories of slogging around in the rain aside, along with our curiosity about what I'd found on the south jetty.

Founder's Day was a big deal in Buck's Landing. Begun in the '50s during the city's centennial celebration, the annual event honored the arrival of Whitney Buck in 1854. He'd sailed into Heron Bay, pushed the Indians aside, and established a redwood mill on the south shore, shipping lumber along the California coast and beyond on schooners like the *C.A. Thayer,* now restored and on display at the Hyde Street Pier in San Francisco. A goodly number of those elegant San Francisco Victorians were built with timber shipped from Heron Bay.

The May event was popular with the locals, a chance to get out of the house after the spring rains, and Squirrel and I looked forward to it every year. The original plan to honor the city's founder had faded somewhat over the years, and nowadays the Founder's Day celebration was more of a street fair, with the Old Town streets closed off and rows of vendors under portable awnings selling local craft items.

Local history might have taken a back seat to commerce over the years, but it was still in evidence. The Old Town fire station rolled out its 1925 Ahrens-Fox engine, proudly displaying the antique pumper with its pin-striped wooden wheels and nickel-plated spotlights and bells. A gent in a beaver hat and tails strolled about, wearing a sandwich board that advertised the open house at the Heritage Society Museum.

The Downtown Merchants Association had a booth with historic photos of Buck's Landing before and after the restoration, and civic groups and local clubs were also represented. The 4-H booth displayed the "Head, Heart, Hands, and Health" motto on a large poster above photographs of youngsters with their animals. The Posey farm was in the background of some of the pictures.

Squirrel and I had arrived early to put up the canopy and set up the folding tables. It was a sunny morning, with a westerly breeze that pushed the sour smell of the pulp mill away from Old Town toward the mud flats at the eastern end of Heron Bay. Teddy showed up a little later, and began putting out brochures that explained the club's goals and provided information on the various 4-H projects available to youngsters. He looked sharp, wearing his "whites," the official dress uniform for members. I was surprised to see him arrive without Dolly, since the two were usually joined at the hip. I wondered if everything was okay between them. She'd been off the crutches for a while now, but things seemed to have cooled between them since Charlie stomped on her foot. I thought she blamed Teddy somehow, but what did I know? Maybe she was still worried about the prom.

Lorna Aguirre showed up at ten-thirty to take her turn in the booth with Bobby Cantwell's mom, who'd arrived a few minutes earlier. Dolly limped along beside her, swinging that walking boot. She looked nice in her white skirt and a crisp white blouse with a collar and the green 4-h club cap, but she didn't look happy.

I looked at Squirrel and nodded toward Dolly and her mother. "What's up with them?" I asked. Squirrel saw the look on Dolly's face and went over to talk to her.

I unboxed more brochures and handed them to Teddy, who was watching Dolly and her mother. I chatted with him as we laid out the folders on the table.

"Looks like we got lucky with the weather," I said. "There's always a chance of rain, even in May."

"Yeah, I remember a couple years back when it poured— really messed up everybody's plans."

"The vendors had just set up when the rain started. Some of them stuck it out for a while, covered their stuff with tarps. When it didn't stop, they finally gave up and folded their tents."

"Don't have to worry about rain today." Teddy looked toward the bay. "Sun's out—even got a little breeze to air out the smell from the mill."

Squirrel returned in a few minutes, a secretive smile on her face. She leaned in close, whispering, "Dolly's mad because she has to wear a skirt. Couldn't get that walking cast on otherwise." *Ah, the feminine mind at work again.*

Teddy walked over to see Dolly. He was all smiles. I don't think that skirt she was wearing bothered him at all.

When the parents had everything in hand, Squirrel and I decided to take in the other sights. She put her arm in mine, and we strolled down the street.

A man at the animal rescue booth was making balloon animals for the children, next to a sign on the table seeking donations. An owl tethered to a pedestal stared unblinking at the passing crowd. I thought it was stuffed at first, until it turned its head, startling me and a young boy who was watching the man turn blue balloons into a dachshund.

A couple decked out in Victorian dress were selling vintage clothing at the next booth, with items from different eras arranged on racks behind their tables. A young couple was browsing their collection. The woman tried on a blue uniform hat with a checkered hatband and a silver badge above the visor. "A British policewoman's hat," the vendor said, holding up a hand mirror. "It looks really great on you."

The top-hatted museum promoter with the sandwich board strolled past us, smiling as he handed Squirrel a folder highlighting the museum's collection. "We haven't been there in years," she said as she glanced through the folder and stuffed it in her purse. "We should take a look. It's just around the corner, across from Vogel's."

"Sure," I said. "Maybe this afternoon."

It was nearing lunchtime as we passed the booths selling local products—artisan raw honey, nut butters, all kinds of flours and grains at one table, wild caught smoked salmon and venison jerky at another. Locally-sourced cheeses and dried fruits and preserves were sold at another table, with samples being handed out by a gray-haired woman in a checked apron. We tried a few, and bought two jars of boysenberry jam. My stomach was grumbling.

"Why don't we get some lunch?" Squirrel said. "I'm starving."

"Me, too," I replied.

We headed down the street, hoping to find an outdoor table at one of the trendy Old Town cafes, when I heard someone call my name. We were nearing the end of the street and passing some booths for community organizations. My appetite had overtaken my civic pride, and I hadn't really been paying attention to the booths we passed.

"Is that you, Billy Barnes?" I turned to find a booth promoting the Native cultural center. It had been years since

I'd seen Earlene Mack, but I recognized her right away. The years had been kind to Pepper's former girlfriend. Except for the gray in her hair and a few crow's feet at the corners of her eyes, she looked great. That young girl who rode the school bus with us when we were kids had become a handsome woman. Squirrel and I walked over to talk to her.

"Good to see you," Squirrel said. "How are you?"

"I'm doing okay, Sorrel. It's been a while since we rode the bus together. Everybody still call you Squirrel?"

"Only Billy these days. It bothered me at first when the other kids started that, but I didn't let them know, and after a while, I got to where I didn't mind. I'm Sorrel Barnes nowadays."

"We all changed, I guess—turned into ourselves. I used to wear all that makeup, thought it made me look special. My father didn't approve, so I waited till I got on the bus. Put my face on before we got close to town and the other kids piled on."

I remembered watching Earlene's daily ritual, putting on the lipstick and blue eye shadow that transformed her into an exotic creature every morning before we got to school.

"Pepper talked me out of that, you know. The white girls teased me about my 'warpaint.'" She frowned and looked away for a moment. "Pepper told me I was just fine without all that. He was the first boy who ever said that to me." She looked away again. "He's been gone a long time now, but I still miss him."

"Me, too," I said, thinking how different things might have been for all of us if Pepper had survived the war. He'd been declared MIA, but that was fifty years ago. He and I had solved the mystery of Roscoe Stapp's disappearance, but Pepper had disappeared, too—and he wasn't coming back.

We talked some more, catching up on things. Squirrel

and I told her about the Posey farm and the 4-H club. Earlene told us about her work at the cultural center with Native issues, things like fishing rights and the repatriation of Native lands. She was also involved in the center's cultural and health and wellness programs.

I was impressed. Earlene was clearly on a mission. There was a light in her eyes that didn't need makeup. Thirty years with junior high kids had toned down my missionary zeal, but Earlene was still fighting the good fight. I'd retired to the Posey farm, but she was still going strong. I admired her for that.

Earlene looked at Squirrel, pointing to her purse. "I see you've got one of those brochures they give out at the museum. You drop in on their open house today?" "Not yet," Squirrel said. "We thought we might stop by after lunch."

"It's an interesting place, got lots of stuff to see. Folks over there think they got time in a bottle, everything there is to know about local history."

There was an odd tone in her voice. I wondered what she was trying to tell us.

Squirrel looked as puzzled as I was. "What do you mean?" she said.

"Just saying, things aren't always what they seem. Most folks don't even know that museum sits on Indian land. Used to be Wiyot land before the white settlers pushed them off."

"I didn't know that, either," I said. "Why haven't we heard that before?"

"It all depends on who's writing the history books," Earlene said. "Dig a little deeper, and you find out all kinds of interesting things." She paused, looking down the street, where the museum was just out of sight around the corner. "Go take a look, see the history museum for yourself. But drop by the cultural center sometime, and I'll tell you the real story about that place."

We talked a while longer before saying our goodbyes and heading to the Eagle's Roost for a much-delayed lunch. The trendy café was decorated in a nautical theme, with cutesy touches like "buoys" and "gulls" on the restroom doors and artfully-draped fishing nets with starfish and glass floats everywhere. Their overpriced but delectable chowder arrived at our table, steaming in sourdough bread bowls. Neither of us said anything for a few minutes. We were both hungry, and we dug in right away.

Touching her napkin to her lips, Squirrel said, "It was nice seeing Earlene again. She's changed a lot since we were kids."

"I think we all have. She seems okay, a lot more sure of herself than she used to be."

"Sure is—all wound up with her work. But she didn't seem all that happy. I can't believe she never got over Pepper. Found someone else, you know?"

"She found something else. She found a cause, devoted all her energy to it. Still does, apparently."

"What was all that about the museum? That 'time in a bottle' business didn't make much sense. Sounded bitter to me."

"I didn't really get it either." I said. "But we haven't been to the museum for years. Why don't we go take a look, see what they've got in there."

We headed up the block to E Street and walked over to Vogel's and across to the museum. The neoclassic building with its marble columns flanking the arched entry was impressive enough on the outside, but I didn't remember much about what was inside. Those school field trips were a long time ago, and all that old timey stuff didn't mean much back then.

Inside the entrance, a row of display cases along the wall was filled with birds—stuffed specimens of local species—beautifully mounted on branches to represent their habitats. Some of the displays even included the birds' nests and eggs.

There were displays of rocks and minerals, antique firearms, and an elaborately carved back bar rescued from a pioneer saloon, with rows of apothecary bottles lining the shelves in front of the mirrors above the marble counter.

A Victorian bedroom held a bed with an elaborately-carved headboard that was eight feet high, a fainting couch, marble-topped dressers, and a rocking chair with petit point cushions beside an infant cradle. Oil paintings and photographs of grim-faced women and children hung from the walls. An elegant Victorian dress graced a mannequin in one corner, with an array of fancy hats on stands on the dresser beside it.

Nautical artifacts—anchors, nets, lobster traps, harpoons, and other sea-faring gear were arranged along the hallway from that room into another, with photos of historic ships and their crews on the walls.

The next room was devoted to the history of local Native American tribes. A long redwood dugout canoe stretched along one wall, with woven reed fish traps and nets on poles displayed beside it. Rows of display cases on another wall held hundreds of artifacts from the Hupa, Wiyot, Yurok, and Karuk tribes. A pair of mannequins in ceremonial dresses decorated with shells and basket hats presided over an array of cooking baskets and utensils for everyday use.

Squirrel went on ahead of me when I stopped to look at a collection of tools that caught my eye. The years working in the hardware store with Dad had made me curious about how things worked and how things were made.

Bows fashioned from yew wood and spears and arrows with flint or obsidian tips were laid out on one shelf in the display case, and elk antler wedges and stone mauls, tools for splitting wood, were shown on another. A third held hide scrapers and tools for smoothing the surface of the dugout canoes as layers were burned away a little at a time to create the desired shape.

What really caught my attention was a display of elk horn spoons made by Hupa men. The pendant I'd found looked like it was made from the same material. The jeweler had polished the elk horn to a high gloss before the stones were mounted, but I was sure it was the same stuff. I looked to see where Squirrel had gone. I wanted to show her what I'd found. When I finally caught up to her, it turned out she'd made a discovery of her own.

11

I found Squirrel standing in front of a wall of display cases filled with Native baskets. All kinds of baskets were laid out on shelves—burden baskets, baskets for cooking, acorn soup baskets, flour trays, baby baskets, basket caps—all neatly displayed with cards identifying the type of basket and the tribe that made it.

My mother'd had a small Hupa trinket basket that she treasured. I kept it on the bookshelf with her collection of rare books. It was very old and very small, only four or five inches across, with a tight-fitting lid. Her basket was very plain, unlike the beautiful baskets on display here. Some of them were quite old. Many of them were trade baskets, but all of them were decorated with traditional designs woven into the basket.

Squirrel was reading a poster on the wall that told about the different patterns on the baskets. The poster was beside a case displaying those basket caps we'd seen on the mannequins in shell dresses. The caps were like cloche hats, sized to fit tightly on the head. The poster explained the designs.

"I found something I wanted to show you," I said. I was eager to tell her about the elk horn spoons I'd discovered.

"Wait a second. I want to read this," she said.

There was no use talking until she was finished. I knew from experience that Squirrel was going to read every label and tag on the exhibits that caught her eye. It was just what she did.

Finally, she looked up, turning her attention to me, "What did you find?"

"I wanted to show you these elk horn spoons I found."

"Really?" She paused for a second. "Wait till you see what I found." She pointed to the poster she'd been reading. "This talks about the designs the Indians used on their baskets. Take a look at this." She pointed to a spot about halfway down the page. "This remind you of anything?"

When I looked where she was pointing, I knew right away what had caught her eye. The poster showed a design called "snake's nose," isosceles triangles that pointed down, wider at the top and stacked one above the other in a repeating pattern.

"It looks just like those onyx stones on the pendant."

"It does, doesn't it? I saw it right away when I looked at the poster."

We took another look at the baskets on display. Most of the designs shown on the poster were represented on the basket caps in the case beside it, including several examples of the "snake's nose" pattern.

The poster said there was an old story about a snake that watched a woman weaving a basket. "Seeing the design, the snake said, 'Here is my design for a basket mark.' But it's not supposed to represent a snake. It's just what it looks like, similar to other designs with colorful names like 'frog's hand' and 'crab claw.'"

When I walked Squirrel back to show her the elk horn spoons, she didn't seem too impressed. "For God's sake, it's not about the spoons," I told her. "Look at what they're made from."

Eventually Squirrel figured out what I was trying to tell her. "It's the same stuff that pendant you found is made of, isn't it?" She paused, looking back toward the case with the baskets. "Well... I think we found out something today. Don't you?"

"Yeah. I'm not sure what it means, but it looks like that pendant is supposed to be an Indian design, that "snake's nose" pattern." I let that sink in for a moment. "You know what I think? I think somebody wanted Vogel's to make something with a Native design, but Native jewelry I've seen doesn't look anything like that. You saw those shell dresses and the strings of dentalium shells they used as money."

"That pendant is really fancy. The elk horn is a Native material, but it's highly polished, unlike your spoons. Onyx is a semiprecious stone, and that box is sterling. The customer who ordered that pendant is either a fan of Indian design or someone proud of his heritage."

"Well," I said, "whoever he was, he was willing to spend quite a bit on it. It must have been important to him."

"Maybe it wasn't a him."

"Maybe so. Sure would be interesting to know the whole story, though."

It was after four when we got back to the street fair. The crowds had drifted away, and the vendors were packing up. After some time wandering the fair on their own, Teddy and Dolly had come back to help break down the 4-H booth. We took down the canopy and the folding tables and put them in Teddy's Scout. He'd bring them back to the farm on his next visit.

Dolly's mother had served her time in the booth and left earlier. Without her around, there was a lot of hand holding and sappy looks between those two. I figured he and Dolly had worked things out. That walking cast wasn't slowing them down at all.

"It was nice to see Earlene again," Squirrel said as we were driving home. "She's really gotten involved with Native causes, hasn't she?"

"Remember when we saw her on the news? That demonstration over fishing rights on the Klamath?"

"That was a couple of years ago, I think."

"Probably so."

We drove along in silence for a little while. I thought about the things Earlene had said. "She seems happy enough," I said, "but I thought there was a kind of undertone, kind of a bitterness that wasn't there when we were kids."

"Well, her work with Native causes might be the reason for that. The Natives have had so much taken away from them. They didn't teach those things when we were in school."

"Maybe that's it," I said. "I just remember that business about things not always being what they seem."

"Yeah, that part about coming by the cultural center to hear the real story about the museum sounded odd to me, too."

"Maybe we should drop by sometime to see what she was talking about."

May was apple blossom time. On a sunny morning, Squirrel and I toured the orchard, her arm in mine as we strolled along under the pink-and-white blossoms. Some of them drifted down on us as we walked between the rows. Bees flitted about here and there, doing their thing. It might have been a scene out of a movie, one of those love stories. Maybe it was, kind of, but we were doing more than enjoying the sights.

For the last few years we'd had trouble with codling moths in the apple orchard. The pests bore into the apples and spoil the fruit. They lay eggs on the apples when they're developing, and the larvae hatch out and chew into the skin. When they mature, they crawl out and drop to the ground to build cocoons. Some turn into moths and fly into the tree canopy to mate.

As nice as it was to walk among the blossoming trees, we were really checking our moth traps to see if the pests were back again this year. We'd hung the sticky, tent-shaped traps here and there in the trees. I took one down to look inside and showed it to Squirrel.

"There don't seem to be as many as there were last year," I said, handing it to her to examine. "I only see a couple. Some of the traps don't seem to have any."

Squirrel peered inside the trap. "I think you're right," she said, frowning. "But we should probably still spray again this year to keep ahead of them."

When she said "we," I knew who she meant. We'd been careful to keep the orchard clean, to pick up the fallen fruit and inspect the wooden apple boxes for cocoons, but the moths could travel a long ways, a mile or more, to find mating sites on trees. Neither of us were fond of using pesticides, and we tried to avoid them as much as we could. That "royal we" meant I'd be spraying the trees as soon as the blossoms had fallen. It was necessary, I knew, but it was my least favorite job, and I wasn't looking forward to it.

May was a busy month on the Posey farm. If we wanted a pumpkin patch in the fall, now was the time to get to work. Squirrel had given the youngest kids gardening lessons in her classroom in the barn. They'd started their pumpkin seeds in little peat pots in March and transferred them to some cold frames I'd made from scrap wood and old windows Squirrel's father had salvaged somewhere and stored in the barn.

I spread a little aged manure from the pile outside the cow shed on the ground under the cold frames, turning the ground every couple of days till it settled. I added several inches of topsoil. When the manure decomposed, it would add a little heat to the soil to protect it from late frosts.

The little plants had come along nicely. They'd had time to "harden off" in the cold frames. We'd propped the windows open during the day to let the plants get used to the air outside, closing them again when the nights were cool, but the days were warmer now, and it was time to plant the pumpkins in the garden.

The kids planted their pumpkins in hills. Squirrel told them they were like pitcher's mounds and showed them how to make little mounds so the plants would drain properly. The little kids were pros at making dirt piles, it turned out, and they were really excited about seeing their pumpkins grow. We, of course, had our own garden to prepare, and we were busy getting that in shape, too.

The last time we'd talked to Emma, she said she hadn't turned up anything more in the *Herald's* archives. I'd kind of lost interest. I figured we'd found out all there was to learn, but once Emma got hold of an idea, she didn't want to let it go. She was still determined to find out more about that fellow they found on the beach.

When Mom's trinket basket on the bookshelf in the front room caught my eye one day, I remembered Earlene's puzzling remark about the "real story" of the heritage society museum. I wondered what that was all about, and why she'd sounded so bitter about things.

I liked Earlene. She'd always seemed so happy when we were kids, smiling as she cuddled up to Pepper on the bus in the mornings. Her life hadn't always been easy, so I guess it was understandable. Still, I wondered what she was trying to say. Maybe when we weren't so busy, we'd drop by the cultural center and find out.

12

Emma and Frank had invited us to their house for dinner. They lived on H Street in one of the tonier neighborhoods in Buck's Landing. When the city fathers drew the grid for the city in the 1850s, H and I Streets were intended to be important—seventy-five foot-wide boulevards compared to the sixty-foot-wide streets planned for other residential areas. The area was densely forested at the time, and there was a deep gulley that slowed development until it was filled in.

By the turn of the century, the land had been cleared and the pioneer vision was being realized. The city's horse-drawn trolley rolled past houses being built a mile south of downtown. A city park two blocks long between H and I had been laid out, and an enterprising contractor had built a block-long row of nearly identical, but impressive Dutch Colonial homes on H Street next to the park.

Today, the south end of Mackey Park has a rose garden on the H Street side, across the side street from the row of Dutch Colonials, and a playground with swings and a slide on the I Street side. There's a half court basketball setup and a rec room between the playground and the rose garden. Two baseball diamonds take up the rest of the park. H and I became one-way streets in the 1950s to accommodate increased traffic.

The vacant lots along H Street were filled in over the years with a variety of styles—Eastlake Victorians, post-World War I period revivals, back-to-nature Craftsmans, even a fairytale Norman Revival with a turret entryway.

Emma and Frank lived on H Street across from the north end of Mackey Park. Their house had been built in

1940, adding yet another style to the landscape—Streamline Moderne. It was a distinctive house, the only one of its kind, but it always looked out of place to me, like an ocean liner that had run aground across from the park. It was all curves and horizontal lines, with an iron railing that followed the winding steps up to the entry beside a curved wall of glass brick. The corners of the house were all rounded, and bold horizontal lines reached out on either side of a large "porthole" window in the center of the front wall.

The house had been featured in magazines like *Architectural Digest*, and Frank and Emma were quite happy living there. They'd filled the house with minimalist stuff—a lot of chrome and glass—modern pieces and mid-century modern furniture, like the Heywood Wakefield desk in Frank's upstairs office.

It was an expensive house, the kind of thing Frank would buy—because he could—but it didn't do much for me. I liked Frank, even though he was kind of stuffy. He made a lot of money as an attorney, and he and Emma always had nice things, but I thought he went overboard most of the time. Like that Land Rover. He didn't need an expensive car like that to drive from his office to the courthouse, but he bought it because he could. He'd tell you he got it for his fishing trips on the Klamath, but he didn't need a car like that to go on a fishing trip.

I'd fished the Klamath with my dad, standing shoulder-to-shoulder on the bank with other fishermen, having to reel in when someone shouted, "Fish on!" to keep our lines from getting tangled. Frank took along one of his clients, hired a river guide and fished from a 17-foot drift boat with heated seats. He was always gracious and never made me feel small. He and I were as different as Squirrel and Emma, but we got along.

I wasn't sure what kind of attorney Frank was. Something to do with taxes and estates, I thought, but I didn't really know. He didn't talk much about his work, but Emma sometimes complained to Squirrel about the long hours he worked. I thought maybe he had political aspirations.

Dinner at Emma's made me a little nervous. Emma and Frank were relaxed in their fancy surroundings, but all that china and glass made me tense. I was always afraid of breaking something. I was a lot more comfortable having dinner on our farm table with its oilcloth cover.

Squirrel told them about Teddy and Dolly and the disaster with the steer. Everybody chuckled when Squirrel revealed that Dolly was more concerned about missing the prom than she was about the injury to her foot.

"It's been a while since we were their age," Emma said. "Little things were such a big deal back then."

"True enough," Frank said. "I remember I couldn't wait to turn eighteen, thought I'd have arrived when I got to be that old." He looked across the table and smiled. "Funny thing, though, now I don't really remember much about that time. Too much's happened since then."

Eventually Emma brought up the subject of the south jetty incident and her attempts to find information on that Whitehorse fellow.

"Like I said, I couldn't find him in the phone book or in the *Herald's* obituaries, but not everything gets into the newspaper. Searching online didn't get me anywhere either."

"We haven't given it much thought, I'm afraid," Squirrel said. "We had other things to deal with—all that drama with Teddy and Dolly, for one thing."

Frank glanced at Emma. "I tried to suggest that this guy was from somewhere else, but Emma doesn't think so. I dunno—lots of men came here during the war."

Emma pursed her lips, thinking. "I suppose it's possible. Obviously, we don't really know much. I've been busy at the paper. Maybe somebody should check in the recorder's office, look into the property records, see if anything pops up."

"Billy and I may have found something," Squirrel said. "Not about the man on the beach, though. But we stopped in at the museum on Founder's Day."

"It's about the pendant I found on the beach—the one we showed you," I said. Squirrel gave me a withering look. "Sorry for interrupting—go ahead."

"As I was saying," she continued, "we went to the museum to take a look at what they had. We hadn't been in there in years."

Squirrel explained about the room housing all the local Native exhibits and what we'd found there. "That 'snake's nose' basket design is just like the stones on the pendant, those triangles one above the other, and the elk horn utensils are made from the same thing the stones are mounted on."

Nobody said anything for a minute or two. Finally Emma spoke up. "That's really interesting. That design is very distinctive. If you found it on those baskets, there has to be some local connection. Why pick that design otherwise? It's unlikely to be a coincidence, if you ask me."

"Maybe," Frank offered, "somebody just liked Indian designs. You know, like those armband tattoos some people get, the ones that look like a bracelet, with feathers and everything."

"Those things are pretty stupid," Emma said. "I don't think they have much to do with real Native traditions."

"Just saying," Frank said. He looked a little sheepish. "Since you found that on the beach where the guy got beat up, maybe it's all connected somehow."

"You might look into the county records," Emma said,

"see if you can find anything."

Squirrel gave me a look. "We're kind of busy at the farm right now, but that might be worth trying."

"I remember my chats with Dottie Taylor when I was looking into the Roscoe Stapp disappearance years ago. She was pretty helpful. I don't know who's running the show down there now," I said, "but it would be something to try."

Squirrel looked at Emma. "We ran into Earlene Mack at the street fair on Founder's Day. You remember Billy's friend Pepper? Earlene was his girlfriend back then. Anyway, she's all involved in Native issues these days. She told us to visit the museum, but drop by to see her at the cultural center if we wanted to learn the 'real story' behind that place. Kind of an odd thing to say, I thought, but maybe we could show the pendant to her and see what she thinks about the design."

"Good idea," I said. "But I still want to know what she meant by 'the real story' of the museum." I put air quotes around 'the real story.'"

"Me, too," Squirrel said. "We should find time to go see her."

"Let us know what she says," Emma said. "It wouldn't hurt to take another run at the beach with that metal detector, either."

I had been putting off dealing with those codling moths, but "we" still had to get after them, so one day when the sun was out and there was little wind, I hooked up the spray rig Russ had made to the tractor. Always improvising, Russ had made a trailer from an old pickup bed and built a wooden tank that fit inside. A gas-powered pump mounted on the tongue provided enough pressure to reach the highest limbs on the trees.

I poured in some Malathion and filled the tank with

water. Russ had built in a paddle on the cover of the tank. The handle stuck up through a hole in the cover and pivoted on a length of pipe mounted across the opening. I pushed the handle back and forth for a few minutes to mix up the pesticide. I didn't like using the stuff, but if we were ever going to be rid of those codling moths, it was a necessary chore. I put on a pair of safety glasses and donned a mask, meager protection but better than nothing.

I drove into the orchard, stopping between the trees to hit them with the spray. It would have been easier with two people, one to drive the tractor and one to do the spraying, but Squirrel's "we" didn't really mean we. It wasn't a fun job, but there was no need for both of us to be around that stuff.

With the spraying done, I had a little time to think about what Emma'd said that night after dinner. She'd been pretty excited when she found those articles in the *Herald's* archives, but not finding anything after that had taken the edge off her curiosity. She wasn't one to give up easily; I thought she might still come up with something. I knew her work at the paper kept her busy. Maybe it was time "we" did some looking ourselves.

Following Emma's suggestion, I tossed my Minelab Explorer SE Pro into the trunk of my car the next day and headed out to the south jetty. Squirrel didn't want to come along. She claimed she had too much to do at home—laundry and such—but I think she just said that. She knew I was getting antsy, and it was time for me to have a little time to myself, to "get out there and blow the stink off," as she liked to say.

It was a sunny day, but the wind was up, and the smell of the pulp mill hit me as soon as I stepped out of the car. As usual, there didn't seem to be anybody around. It was a weekday, so I didn't expect company. Squirrel had reminded me to take my phone with me—just in case. The south beach was a pretty lonely spot, but I wasn't worried about bad guys showing up. If anything, I was more likely to fall in a hole and twist my ankle, ending up like Dolly with one of those walking boot things. I didn't think there were any cell towers nearby anyway.

The spit leading out to the jetty hadn't yielded much my first time out, but I decided to head down that way and work my way back to the car. There was nary a beep or boop from my SE Pro, but I plodded along anyway, disturbing a pair of seagulls squabbling over an empty crab shell that had washed up on the shore. They flew off, wheeling above me for a moment before drifting east over the bay.

I was about to pack it in as I neared the parking area when I saw the cut in the dunes where I'd found that silver box in the old streambed and decided to look over there again. The rain had sluiced some more dirt from the bank, but nothing set off the metal detector. I waved the search coil all around that spot, but there was still nothing. I gave up and headed back to the car.

The road used to run out to the end of the jetty before they put up that gate and closed the beach. I climbed the bank and walked along the old road. It wasn't much more than a trail now, overgrown with dune grass. As the road curved away from the beach to begin the climb up the hill to the bluff, I heard a beep from the metal detector. I found a stick and poked around in the dirt at the edge of the road. Where the turn was sharpest, there was dirt and sand piled up at the outside edge. The beeps were loudest there.

I dug down in the piled-up dirt at the edge of the road, hitting something solid a few inches into the pile. I got down on my hands and knees, clearing away the dirt. There was something down there, something curved and shiny. I cleared away more of the dirt and pushed the stick in under the edge of the thing and pried it up out of the dirt.

It was only a hubcap from an old car, probably lost when the car had driven hard into the turn, distorting the wheel enough to make the cap fly off. I'd lost a couple of hubcaps off my Chevy that way. I hadn't expected to find much of anything this time, but at least I hadn't got skunked.

I turned the hubcap right side up and smacked it on the ground to knock out the dirt packed inside. I wiped the dirt off the shiny side to see if it said anything. The word "Graham" was stamped across the center of the hubcap. I knew that was an old car brand, one that hadn't been around for years. It was a curiosity, something to show Squirrel. When I got back to the car, I wiped it off in the dune grass, cleaned up the inside a little more, and tossed it in the trunk with the metal detector.

13

Squirrel wasn't impressed when I told her what I'd found beside the road. She looked at me with a silly grin. "Can't all be gems, I guess."

"Oh—ha ha—very funny," I said.

"Well, you didn't really expect to find anything else out there, did you?"

"Not really. It was Emma who suggested it might be worth going out there again."

"Yeah. Well, at least it gave you an excuse to get out of the house, play with that detector thing she thought you should have."

"It is kind of fun to play with, but next time I'll go somewhere else. I think I'm done with the south jetty beach."

When we were getting ready to go into town a week later to pick up some mash and crumble to feed the chickens, Squirrel suggested we take along the onyx pendant and show it to Earlene. We could also find out what she was trying to tell us about the museum. I was just as curious as Squirrel was. It seemed like a good idea.

Olsen's feed store had been supplying farmers in the surrounding area since the 1890s. The building with its wide loading dock out front hadn't changed since Squirrel and I were kids. We pulled into the parking area in front of the loading dock and went inside the office. Dean, the current Olsen running the store, greeted us as we came in. After we ordered some chicken mash, some layer crumble, and shell grit, we chatted a bit with Dean and then headed out to the loading dock.

Squirrel and I climbed the steps beside the dock and walked into the warehouse. A young man in a green work apron was wheeling a pallet jack loaded with sacks of fertilizer into place next to another. He stopped what he was doing when he looked up and saw us.

I handed him our receipt, and he headed into the back to get what we wanted. We waited near the front, looking around at all the stuff in the warehouse.

"I used to love coming here with my dad," Squirrel said. "I still do. It's all the alfalfa and the grain, the way it smells. I love it."

"Me, too," I said. I knew what she meant. Our barn was kind of like that, but it wasn't quite the same. Olsen's always had that fresh, clean smell of hay and cedar shavings. Maybe Flossie's manure pile outside the cow shed explained the difference.

The young guy returned with our feed sacks on a hand truck and wheeled them out to the edge of the dock. I backed the car up and he stepped down and placed the sacks into the trunk. He returned the receipt and we drove off.

The Heron Bay Cultural Center was located in the Mackey building on Third and F, just a block up from Vogel's. It was an elaborate three-story affair built by Noah Mackey with his timber fortune. It had a brick façade with terra cotta tile decorations and turrets on the upstairs corners. When Squirrel and I were kids, it had been stuccoed over, obscuring most of the decorative elements, and the corner turret on the west side had been removed, replaced by a tall sign for the appliance store that rented the space. It was just an old gray building as long as I could remember. It was certainly different now.

The glass block panels installed above the first floor

storefront windows had been removed and replaced with clear glass, restoring the original look. The green-painted trim contrasted with the red brick and the terra cotta tile decoration on the Third Street side.

The entrance to the cultural center was on the corner, under the restored turret where the appliance store's buzzing neon sign had hung when Squirrel and I were kids. An upscale clothing store was on one side of the entrance, and a fancy wine merchant had opened a shop on the other side.

We found a parking space across the street, crossed at the corner, and entered the center. Inside, visitors were greeted with the inevitable gift shop, with shelves of books on Native history and glass display cases with local crafts for sale, mostly jewelry.

Behind the counter on the back wall was a colorful rendition of the Heron Bay logo, a red outline map of the bay with a blue heron wading in the shallows. The border was decorated with Indian designs, the same ones we'd seen on the baskets in the museum. The snake's nose pattern was prominent among them.

Beside the colorful logo was a large poster listing all the services offered at the center: educational services, community health and wellness programs, employment training, legal services, youth programs, and others. I was still reading the list when a young woman entered from a side door and stepped behind the counter.

"Good morning," she said, "Can I help you folks with something?"

Squirrel'd been looking at some of the items in the jewelry case and stepped up beside me. "Hi," she said. "We were hoping to see Earlene Mack. Is she here today?"

"She was in her office earlier. If you give me your names, I'll check for you."

"We're Sorrel and Billy Barnes. We talked to Earlene on Founder's Day."

She picked up a headset on the back counter, slipped it on, and punched a button on the desk phone. "Some folks named Barnes are here to see you," she said. There was a pause as she listened for a moment. "Okay, sure," she said. She took off the headset, putting it back on the counter. "Earlene's in her office." She pointed to the doorway she'd come through earlier. "Just go down the hall. Her office is the first one on the right."

We thanked her and went through the doorway. One side of the hallway was hung with large posters showing the great seals of local tribes: Wiyot, Yurok, Karuk, and Hupa. The opposite wall had framed color photographs of tribal council members. One of them caught my eye. It was a photo of an attractive woman, with dark-rimmed glasses, smiling at the camera. What made me notice her was the "111" tattoo on her chin.

I pointed at the picture. "I didn't think they did that anymore."

Squirrel looked where I was pointing. "Some people must be reviving the old traditions."

We'd both seen historical photos of local Indians with the three vertical lines tattooed on their chins. My mother told me she'd seen them on some old folks when she was a girl, but I'd never seen those marks on a real person. "It sure looks that way," I said as we made our way down the hall.

Earlene looked up from her desk when we tapped on the open door. "Billy, Sorrel—hi. Come on in." She pointed to a pair of chairs facing the desk. "Have a seat. It's nice to see you again. I was wondering if you'd drop by."

"The farm's been keeping us pretty busy," I said. "But what you said about the museum, that stuff about the 'real story,' got us wondering what you meant."

Earlene frowned, pursed her lips. "It's a long story, one most people don't know. The museum's a nice place to visit, I guess. I told you it sits on Indian land, but there's a move on to work out a deal with the Wiyot tribe to make the place more socially responsible. They've given back some items in the collection, stuff that was stolen, but it's the history of the place that bothers me."

I glanced at Squirrel. She looked as puzzled as I was. "What do you mean?" she asked.

"The museum started as a private collection. All those stuffed birds in there were part of it. A local woman, a history teacher—white of course—started collecting Indian artifacts, too. Baskets and things. In the 1930s she got like-minded people to help her. They dug up burial grounds in the area, saying they were 'preserving local history.'"

She pointed to a picture on the wall, one I'd seen before. It was a sepia tone photograph of an Indian spearfishing on the Trinity. It was from Edward Curtis' 20-volume series *The North American Indian*. My mother had tried unsuccessfully for years to acquire even one of the rare books. Nowadays the pictures were readily available on line.

"You know about that fellow Curtis, who took all the pictures of Native Americans?"

"Mom told me about him," I said. "She was a librarian, interested in old books."

"Yeah," Earlene said. "Well, he wanted to photograph what he called 'the vanishing Indian.' He made nice pictures, but sometimes he cheated a little, dressing Indians up in costumes that were all wrong, posed them in ways that weren't natural."

Earlene turned away from the picture, looked at us with a sad smile. "Funny thing is, they're the only pictures we have of a lot of our ancestors." She paused for a moment before continuing.

"At least, the only thing he took was pictures. The history teacher dug up the bones of our people, sold them to collectors, and shipped them off to museums. That fellow in the picture is a Yurok, a man from my tribe—probably one of my ancestors. How would you like it if your great-grandfather's skull was tagged and numbered and sitting on a shelf in a Sacramento museum?"

I looked at Squirrel, then turned back to Earlene. "Wow—we had no idea. No one ever told us any of this."

"We don't learn everything in school. Sometimes the teachers don't even realize how they're passing along ideas. Remember Miss Palmer at the Prairie Creek school?"

"Sure," Squirrel said. "What about her?"

Earlene and Squirrel had known each other since kindergarten. They'd gone to the one-room elementary school before my family moved from town. The school only went to the eighth grade, and I'd been too old by the time we moved. I didn't meet them till I started riding the bus to school in town.

"Remember that "Ten Little Indians" rhyme she taught us? Squirrel pursed her lips, a puzzled look on her face. "Of course. She taught us to count when we were little. 'One little, two little, three little Indians'—like that."

"Remember how the nursery rhyme ends?"

Squirrel looked away, counting on her fingers. "It's 'one little Indian boy,' I think."

"That was Miss Palmer's version. But other versions end with 'And then there were none.' Nobody thinks anything about it, but it's part of that 'vanishing Indian' notion that people like Curtis promoted."

"I learned that rhyme when I was little, too," I said. "I

never thought anything of it."

"Most people don't. It's part of the coded historical narrative that passes on the ideologies of older generations."

"That's a real eye-opener, Earlene. You've really given us something to think about."

"I liked Miss Palmer, too. She was just teaching us to count. She didn't know there was any more to it than that. Kids nowadays learn 'one little, two little' fingers—or puppies or cookies." She smiled, "Anything but Indians."

"We don't find out everything in school, I guess," I said. "We still have a lot to learn."

"The history books don't tell the whole truth. Rich and powerful people know how to keep their secrets hidden— say grave robbers are 'preserving history.' What we know depends on who's telling the story. Indigenous peoples have been here for thousands of years, but we weren't uniformly granted citizenship until 1924. We're still working to maintain our sovereignty and fighting over treaty-granted rights."

"Well," Squirrel said, "you've certainly got your work cut out for you. But it sounds like you're making progress. Thanks for telling us about the museum's history. You've given us a lot to think about. We'd never heard any of that before."

"Most people haven't. The ones who have don't seem to care. It's old news, stuff that happened a long time ago." Earlene looked at us, gave us another sad smile. "Some of us know where all the bodies are buried—or at least where they used to be."

We were silent for a moment or two while we let that sink in. I knew we weren't responsible for any of that, but I could hear the hurt in her voice, and I felt embarrassed somehow.

Finally, Squirrel changed the subject, reaching into her

pocket. There's something else we wanted to ask to you about."

Just then, the phone on Earlene's desk rang. "Excuse me," she said, picking up the receiver. "Hello, this is Earlene." There was a long pause while she listened. "When was this?" she said. "I'll be right over. Don't say anything till I get there."

Earlene hung up and turned to us. "I'm going to have to cut our visit short. One of our young men just got picked up by the cops. He's a good kid, but he hangs out with rough types sometimes. He says he wasn't doing anything, but he needs some help. I need to run over there and see what's going on." She stood up, grabbing her coat from the back of her chair. "I'm sorry. We can talk some more later."

Squirrel and I thanked her and followed her as she rushed down the hall ahead of us. As we crossed the street to the car, Squirrel pulled the silver box from her pocket. She looked my way and frowned. "Too bad she had to rush off before we could ask her about this."

"Maybe next time," I said.

14

Squirrel said, "We need to do something about it, Billy." She turned the kitchen faucet wide open. "Just look at this!"

Squirrel was trying to wash the breakfast dishes, but the water coming out of the faucet was only a trickle. The pressure switch on the pump in the tankhouse had gotten balky in the past few weeks. When the water pressure dropped, the switch was supposed to turn on the pump to maintain pressure in the lines, but lately it was refusing to cooperate. I'd changed over to the old system of gravity feed from the tank, but the water pressure was not what we were used to. If the pump didn't work and we ran out of water in the tank, we wouldn't have any water at all.

A few judicious taps on the plastic housing had freed up the switch a few times, but that didn't last very long. Taking the cover off and cleaning the corroded contacts had worked for a while longer, but the switch was acting up again. The setup was over thirty years old and needed replacing. I'd been putting it off, but when Squirrel said "we need to do something," I knew it was time to get the job done.

"I know," I said. "I'll try to fix it today. But I'll have to go to town to get a new switch. That old one is no good anymore."

I could usually fix things by improvising with something we had on hand, but some projects just required new stuff, and that meant a trip to town.

Bailey's Supply on B Street had been in business forever, but their inventory had evolved with the times, and they had things you couldn't get from the "helpful hardware folks" at Ace. I liked the old building, with its high tin ceiling and oiled wood floors. The thing about Bailey's was that if you wanted a fine thread carriage bolt or a couple of finishing washers, you could buy what you needed without having to buy eight or ten pieces sealed in a plastic bag. They also had a guy who seemed to know everything about plumbing.

EJ was a black fellow who had worked at Bailey's as long as I could remember. He was probably in his eighties now, but still going strong. I thought I was old when I saw myself in the mirror these days, but talking to EJ made me feel a little like I had when I went in there as a kid to stock up on BBs for my Daisy air rifle. A lot of things had changed since then. It was comforting to know places like Bailey's were still around.

EJ had lost his right leg long before I knew him, but he'd always gotten around fine on crutches. His short cropped hair was nearly white now. There were some age spots on his cheeks, and his face had a few more lines than I remembered, but he looked good for his age. You didn't ask EJ for help if you were in a hurry, but if you had a plumbing problem, it was worth waiting for him. I'd tried to fix stuff on my own before, ending up buying parts that didn't fit or things I didn't need, but EJ had never steered me wrong. I always got just what I needed and had nothing left over when the job was done.

I found EJ in the back of the store. He was perched on a stool, his crutches leaning against the shelves where he was stocking different-sized copper pipe fittings into bins. He wore a chambray shirt and Ben Davis jeans held up with wide suspenders. The right leg was cut short and sewn up.

I pulled the old pressure switch out of my pocket to show him what I needed. EJ took the switch from me, pushed his gold-rimmed glasses up, and studied it carefully.

"This here pretty old," he said, turning it over in his hands.

I thought he was going to tell me I was out of luck, but Bailey's had been around for years. I figured the folks at Ace would tell me to go online and order the switch or maybe offer to put in a special order, but I was banking on EJ to come through for me.

"Gimme a minute," EJ said. "Lemme see what I can find." He slid off the stool, got his crutches under his arms, and made his way further back into the store. I followed along in case he came up with something. I didn't want him to have to walk all the way back to where I'd met up with him.

EJ went behind a back counter where long rows of shelves held all kinds of small parts. He disappeared down one of the rows. I leaned against the counter while I waited. I hoped he'd find a switch that would work. I didn't want to have to go searching from one place to another.

If I didn't have to spend all afternoon running from pillar to post, I thought maybe I'd drop into the County Recorder's Office and look up that Whitehorse fellow. Emma had thought there might be something in the birth and death records or the property records to shed some light on who he was.

I was about ready to give up when EJ reappeared with a small box tucked under his arm.

"Looks like you found something," I said, as he put the box on the counter and began to open it.

"This be the same as your switch," he said, taking the switch out of the box and setting it on the counter beside mine. "Changed the shape and such over the years, but it's the same switch. Mounting holes in the same place as yours. Should work just fine." He looked up at me and smiled, "Just bring it back if it don't."

I thought there was a little joke there. I knew most electrical parts couldn't be returned.

"I'm not worried," I said. "You've never steered me wrong before. That's why I come here when I need something."

"The boss keep me around 'cause I know a little bit about things. I try to help people. Some folks show me pictures on they phones when they want something. That work sometimes, but a lot of folks go on they computer now when they want something. Hard to ask questions if you don't know what you lookin' for. Thanks for stoppin' by. Just glad I could help."

I thanked EJ and took the new switch to the front counter and paid for it. I left Bailey's, relieved that I wasn't going to have to run all over town to find a switch or, worse yet, have to go online. I got into the car and headed to the courthouse.

The Recorder's Office was in the basement of the courthouse. I'd been there before when Pepper and I were looking into the disappearance of Roscoe Stapp. Mom worked at the library back then, and her friend Dottie Taylor ran the Recorder's Office. The library was in a new building now, one of the many changes as Buck's Landing grew over the years.

County records were still kept in the courthouse basement, but things in that office had changed. The shelves on the back wall were still lined with the tall leather-bound ledgers I remembered, their labels dating back to the 1800s. That was about the only thing I recognized.

Several desks behind the counter were equipped with computer monitors and occupied by clerks who were clacking away on keyboards. Entering the office had set off a chime, and one of the clerks, a young woman, looked up from her work when I entered. She left her desk and came to the counter.

"Good afternoon," she said. "What can I help you with

today?'

I was a little adrift. This thirty-something woman wasn't at all like Dottie Taylor, with reading glasses dangling from her neck and gray hair tied up in a bun. I felt a bit like I did when I went to see the doctor nowadays and was met by someone young enough to have been one of my students.

I tried to ignore the tattoos on her neck and the eyebrow piercings. "I wanted to look into any records you might have for a man called Jacob Whitehorse. You know—property records, birth and death, that kind of thing."

"Sure, we can do that," she said, smiling. She pulled a sheet from the organizer at the end of the counter and slid it across the counter to me. "Just fill out this form, and we'll see what we can find for you." She nodded in the direction of a table in the corner. "If you like, you can fill it out over there, or take it home and bring it back later."

I thanked her and headed over to the corner. I sat down, took out my reading glasses, and looked over the form. It included a list of fees for the services the office provided. Dottie hadn't charged anything, probably considering it a favor for my mother, but nobody worked for free these days. The fee for a routine search was thirty dollars. If they found anything, there was an additional charge for a printout. Birth and death certificates were additional as well.

"In for a penny, in for a pound," as Mom used to say. It might be worth paying to see what they came up with. I filled out the form, requesting birth and death information and any records of property ownership the county had on file.

When I returned to the counter, the young woman was no longer at her desk. Another clerk saw me standing there and came over. This one had a purple streak in her hair. "Can I help you?" she said.

I held out the paper and nodded in the direction of the

empty desk. "Another clerk gave me this form to fill out."

"Tiffany's gone to lunch. I can help you with that." She scanned the sheet for a moment. In the space at the bottom marked "for office use only," she initialed the form and stamped the date. She looked up at me and smiled, "There's a thirty-dollar fee."

I handed her my debit card. She used the machine on the counter to charge me and stapled the receipt to the form. "Would you like a copy?" she asked.

I said I did and put it in my wallet when she handed it to me with my card.

"We ask you to give us two weeks to process your request. We will notify you by mail of our findings. Anything else I can do for you?"

"That's all for now," I said. I thanked her and headed back to the car, wondering how perfectly nice-looking people thought tattoos and purple hair made them more attractive.

When I got home, Squirrel was in the kitchen, filling the coffee pot from the puny stream coming from the faucet. She was happy to see me set the box with the new switch on the table. "I'm glad they didn't have to order one. I didn't want to have to wait for a couple of weeks, with the water pressure the way it is—or isn't."

"I know what you mean. Fortunately Bailey's had a switch that will work. EJ had to hunt around, but he found one in the back. I don't know what the store will do without him. He knows just about everything when it comes to plumbing."

Squirrel raised an eyebrow. "Emma'd tell you not to worry. She'd say you can find anything you want online."

"That's her answer for everything."

Squirrel scooped coffee into the percolator basket and inserted it into the pot. She put on the lid and set the pot on the stove. "You were gone quite a while. I thought you were probably having trouble finding what you wanted."

"I should have called. When I got the switch without having to run around town, I decided to stop in at the Recorder's Office to see what they could dig up on that Whitehorse fellow."

Squirrel turned on the burner under the pot and sat down beside me at the table. "That was another of Emma's suggestions. She's just trying to be helpful."

"I know," I said, pausing to think for a moment. "She'd like the Recorder's Office these days, all computers and thirty-somethings tapping away on keyboards. They've still got the old ledger books on the shelves, but I think they're just for show."

"Did you find out anything while you were there?"

"Not exactly. The clerk just handed me a form to fill out and charged me thirty dollars. We're supposed to give them a couple of weeks to see what they can find. They'll send us something in the mail."

Squirrel put her hand on mine and smiled. "Better than waiting a couple of weeks for a new pressure switch to come in the mail. I'm tired of waiting on the water."

15

I'd managed to replace the switch on the pump before our garden started to suffer, and things were back to normal. Squirrel had stopped complaining, and the plants were coming along nicely. We put out onion sets and planted tomatoes we'd started in the cold frames, the Early Girl and Better Boy varieties that were good producers. We planted squash and zucchini, too. They weren't my favorites on the table, but they always grew really well, which was gratifying.

We also planted a row of heirloom pole beans, the purple pod variety that was my favorite, with the purple flowers that are very showy against the green leaves and the long deep purple pods that magically turn green when they're cooked. The tendrils were already starting to twine around the poles.

We planted a few rows of corn, too, but we'd never had much luck with corn. We were too near the coast, with too few hot days, and we had to struggle with the raccoons that crept into the garden at night to help themselves. The light I mounted on top of a post was meant to discourage them, but anything that grew in the shadows didn't stand a chance. Still, the tasseled rows are attractive. What's a garden without a few rows of corn?

My trip to the Recorder's Office had been a waste of time and money. The notice we eventually received in the mail informed us that they were unable to locate anyone with that name in their birth, death, or property records. It was another dead end. Still, that made us even more curious. Who was this Jacob Whitehorse fellow? Where had he come from? How could he just disappear?

We weren't getting anywhere, and it didn't seem as if we ever would. Emma gave us a hard time about our obsession with finding out what happened on the south jetty. She said it was okay for me to dig around on the beach with the toy she'd given me, but uncovering the past was a different thing altogether. "You should just let it go," she said.

I had to admit that the thirty dollars I'd wasted at the Recorder's Office had dampened my zeal a bit, but Squirrel was more determined than ever.

With the garden in and the water system back to normal, we had a little time on our hands. Squirrel suggested we give Earlene a call. She'd had a lot to say about the history of the museum, but she'd had to rush off before we had a chance to ask her about the pendant. We were still anxious to see what she had to say about that.

When Squirrel called the cultural center, the receptionist put her on hold for a few minutes. "Earlene's on another line," Squirrel said, putting her hand over the mouthpiece. She pulled the cord over from the phone on the wall and sat down at the kitchen table.

I stood at the kitchen sink, looking out the window. The late morning sun behind the house cast shadows on the front lawn. In the distance a flatbed pickup with a precarious-looking load of hay drove past on the county road.

When Squirrel finally said, "Hi, Earlene. It's Sorrel Barnes," I turned away from the view outside. Squirrel listened for a moment. "Oh, that's okay. I know you're busy." She listened again, nodding her head as if Earlene could see. "I remember," she said. There was another pause as Earlene said something else.

Finally Squirrel said, "I don't want to bother you if you're too busy, but Billy and I wanted to ask you about something we found. When that young man called, you had to leave, and we didn't get a chance."

Squirrel nodded her head as she listened some more. "Sure," she said. "That will be fine. We're looking forward to seeing you again." She said goodbye and stood, placing the receiver back on the cradle.

"Earlene's still trying to help that young man who got in trouble. She said she's going to be busy all morning, but she thought she'd be back in the office after two. I told her that would be fine."

"I know," I said. "I heard your end of the conversation. She say anything else?"

"No. She sounded preoccupied. I expected her to ask what we found that she might know something about, but she kind of cut me off—said something about having to get over to the courthouse."

After lunch, Squirrel and I drove into town to see Earlene. Traffic slowed as we entered Buck's Landing. We crept along behind a logging truck, its twin stacks snorting black smoke as the driver shifted gears through downtown, headed toward the mills on the other side of the bay.

I turned off the main highway when we reached E Street, happy to get out from behind the truck. I turned right when I got to Vogel's corner and drove up the block to the Mackey building on Third and F. We parked at the curb across the street from the cultural center. I waited on the sidewalk while Squirrel dug into her purse for some change to feed the parking meter.

Seeing her rooting around in her purse made me think. "You didn't forget the pendant, did you?"

"No, silly—it's in my pocket." She patted the pocket of her jacket as she stuffed a couple of dimes in the meter.

We crossed the street and entered the cultural center. The

young woman we'd spoken to before was behind the counter. She looked up at us and smiled. "Good afternoon. Nice to see you again."

I was surprised she remembered us, but I suspected Earlene had told her we were coming in.

"Earlene's in her office, but she's with someone. I'll let her know you're here. She shouldn't be too long. "

"We know she's busy," Squirrel said. "We don't mind waiting."

We looked around at the items in the gift shop. Display cases featured handcrafted items from local artists—small baskets, elkhorn spoons similar to the ones in the museum, and lots of jewelry. Squirrel pored over the jewelry, which was surprising to me, since she seldom wore jewelry other than her wedding band.

She pointed to a silver ring inlaid with coral. "Everything is beautifully made," she said. "Look at this, Billy." She pointed to a pair of earrings, each with three triangular pieces separated by beads. The triangles pointed down, like the ones on our pendant. I didn't know what they were made of, but the pieces were a warm amber color and highly polished. Squirrel was right. They were beautifully made.

After a few minutes, a young man came out of the hallway that led to the offices. He looked to be in his thirties, with dark hair worn long and tucked behind his ears. He had on blue jeans and a plaid flannel shirt open over a white T-shirt. Earlene had her arm around his shoulder. He looked down, his head tipped toward her as she talked to him, too softly for me to hear what she was saying. He had a sheet of paper in his hand.

They stopped at the counter, and Earlene took her arm off his shoulder and pointed to the paper. I heard her say, "Go down there now. They're expecting you. You have to stay out of trouble from now on."

The young man looked at Earlene and nodded. He headed our way, head down, across the gift shop. He didn't look happy, more like resigned, the way I felt when I went to the dentist.

Earlene looked after him, smiled when she saw us, and gestured for us to come over. We followed her down the hall toward her office. As we walked along, she explained. "That was Lonnie, one of my charges. He can't stay out of trouble, hangs out with the wrong crowd. He got picked up with some other guys, but he wasn't really doing anything.

"I've got a friend on the docks who believes in second chances. The judge agreed to let Lonnie off with probation if he promised to work for my friend. A couple of months as a lumper, unloading fish and stacking cargo, should give him time to think. All Lonnie needs is a job, something to do, you know?"

I put in my two cents' worth as we sat down in Earlene's office. "I remember my dad telling me, 'Work is edifying.' He said it made me a better person. He was always finding me jobs, usually crummy jobs like pulling weeds in somebody's yard, but I know what you're saying. I think my dad knew what he was talking about."

"I just hope Lonnie gets the message," Earlene said. "He needs to take hold somewhere." She paused, shifted gears, and looked at Squirrel, smiling. "When you called, you said you wanted to ask me about something you found. I was really busy and didn't have time to think about it, but now I'm curious. What was that all about?"

Squirrel fished in her pocket. "Billy has one of those metal detector things. He drove out to the beach on the south jetty to try it out."

"That wouldn't have been my first choice," Earlene said.

"There's not much to see out there. Hardly anyone visits the south jetty. The beaches up north are a lot more interesting. I wouldn't expect you'd find much."

"I like to get out by myself sometimes," I said. "I wanted to try out my new toy without a bunch of people watching."

"Well," Earlene said smiling, "you picked the right place for that." She pursed her lips, looking away for a second. "Remember all the stories we heard about that place?"

"Of course," Squirrel said. "Our parents always warned us to stay away—told us there'd been a murder out there." Squirrel took the silver box out of her pocket and set it on the desk. "After Billy found this, my sister Emma, who works at the *Herald*, dug into the archives and found a couple of articles about what really happened. The story turned out to be a little different than what our parents told us."

"It usually is," Earlene said. She reached across the desk and pulled the box closer.

"According to the stories in the paper," Squirrel continued, "a young couple was attacked on the beach at night. The man was badly beaten and left for dead, and the woman disappeared. There were only a couple of stories afterward. The sheriff interviewed the man, somebody named Jacob Whitehorse. He claimed he didn't know who attacked them, and he refused to name the woman he was with. There wasn't anything in the paper after that. Emma kept looking, but the story just dried up."

"People like mysteries," Earlene said. "Come up with all kinds of things trying to explain what might have happened." She glanced at the box on the desk. "My father told me about what went on out there, too." She paused, a distant look in her eyes. "That was a long time ago—before our time." She looked at me and smiled, "So, Billy—what's in the box?"

I popped open the box, pulled back the lid, and turned it

around so Earlene could see the pendant inside. She took the pendant out and laid it across her palm.

"This is really beautiful," she said.

"There was muddy water in the box," Squirrel said, "but it cleaned up nicely."

Earlene turned the pendant over and looked at the back. "Looks like it came from Vogel's jewelry store. I remember that little bird trademark."

"That mark's on the box, too," Squirrel said. "On the bottom. We took it down to the store. Karl Vogel said that HV on the pendant is his grandfather's mark. His name was Horst Vogel. Karl found the original invoice, written in German. Karl translated it, said it was a special order—dated 1946."

Earlene turned the pendant over, running her finger over the onyx triangles.

"When we visited the museum on Founder's Day," Squirrel explained, "we saw some baskets with the same pattern. The poster beside the display said that design was called 'snake's nose.' We wanted to ask you what you thought when we visited earlier, but we got to talking, and then you had to rush out."

" It happens sometimes. I didn't mean to be rude."

"We understand," I said. "But after you left, we realized we hadn't gotten a chance to ask you about the pendant. So that's why we're here now."

"Well, I think you're right about the design. It sure looks like that pattern you see on some of the baskets, but it wasn't made by a Native artist. I could tell that even without the Vogel's trademark. Something made that long ago would have a different look. The base is elkhorn, I think. That's something local Indians have used for ages, but the onyx— not so much."

I told Earlene about the drawing that was stapled to the original invoice. "Karl said it was the design the customer brought in when he ordered the pendant."

Earlene traced her finger over the stones again. She looked up at Squirrel. "It's a lovely thing. Vogel's always carries the nicest jewelry. Somebody paid a lot to have something like this made. A gift for someone's lover, maybe."

"Turn it over," Squirrel said. "There's something else on the back."

Earlene picked up a pair of black-framed reading glasses, put them on. "I don't like these things—hate to admit I need them."

"Welcome to the club," I said. "We all need them nowadays."

"We wanted to ask you about those letters on the back," Squirrel said.

She turned the pendant, peered at the writing for a moment. "Well, it's definitely something for a loved one. That word—*niwhdin*—that's a Hupa word. It means 'I'm in love with you,' or something like that."

"How'd you say it?" I asked.

"The i's are short, like fit. The n's and the d's are the same as in English. The hard part is that wh in the middle. It's like the ew sound in few. Ni-ew-din is pretty close, I think. I've learned a little, but I'm hardly an expert."

"Well, that's really interesting," Squirrel said, glancing my way. "We wondered what those letters meant. It makes sense now—the pendant was for a loved one."

A woman stopped in the hall outside the open door. Earlene looked up as she stepped into the doorway. "Sorry to bother you, Earlene. I just wanted to remind you about the meeting this afternoon."

"Thanks, Doris, I'll be there." She glanced at the clock on

the wall. "We've still got half an hour."

When the woman left, Earlene explained. "We're always struggling for recognition. I told you about the museum trying to work out a deal with the Wiyot tribe. There's a move on to rename Mackey Island."

"Isn't there a memorial there now?"

"Yeah. Folks know what went on out there, but it's more than that. Noah Mackey plastered his name on everything he touched. We're sitting in the Mackey Building. There's Mackey Park, Mackey Lane. He built his fancy house out there and claimed the island for his own. But the Indians that were slaughtered out there deserve recognition more than some rich white guy that squatted there after they were dead.

"We've got the memorial, but that place needs another name. A committee is going to the city council with a proposal. They're arguing over the name. Different groups want recognition, but I think they'll just end up calling it Indian Island."

"Better than Mackey Island, I suppose," Squirrel said. "I remember the big house that used to be there. I thought he fell on hard times, let it go to ruin."

"I've heard those stories, too, but that's not really what happened. The truth always comes out if you dig deep enough. Rich folks can hide behind their money, don't want to wash their dirty linen in public. The older generation, our parents, kept secrets, too. When enough time passes and no one is around who remembers, the truth comes out—especially nowadays, with the internet and folks looking into their heritage."

Earlene paused, looking away for a moment before she continued. "Before he died, my father told me a lot I didn't know about our family history. Some of the things I learned surprised me."

Squirrel interrupted Earlene. "You said Mackey didn't really fall on hard times? So what really happened?"

"He lived in that big house on the island with his wife and their daughter. His wife died when she was still young, leaving him to raise the girl. He had an Indian housekeeper to look after her, but she wasn't enough. He was obsessed with the girl, kept her with him all the time, always took her with him when he was away on business, on fishing trips on the Klamath. He never let her out of his sight. When she got older, she wanted to live her own life, escape from that island prison. When he finally died, she moved into town and let the house go, putting all that behind her."

"Wow," I said. "All that happened before we came along. We always thought he just went broke and let the house go. I never even knew he had a daughter. The real story is a lot different."

Earlene put the pendant back in the box and carefully closed the lid. She squinted at the design on the top for a moment. Her mouth twisted and a line appeared between her brows. She pushed the box back across the desk, looking up at the clock on the wall. "It always is," she said.

16

We knew Earlene was in a hurry to get to her meeting. As she gathered some papers from her desktop and stuffed them in a manila folder, we thanked her for telling us what she could about the pendant, told her we could find our way out, and headed back to our car.

Neither of us said anything for a while as we drove through downtown. When we were passing Olsen's feed store on the outskirts of Buck's Landing, Squirrel said, "Earlene was certainly helpful, wasn't she? She knew right away what that word meant. That surprised me—shows how much she's learned."

She turned toward me as I glanced her way. "The pendant was a love token, a gift for someone special."

"Sure seems like it," I said. "She didn't say anything about that J under the word, though."

"Maybe she didn't see it. She needs her reading glasses as much as we do."

The coastal fog that was with us night and morning in the summer was beginning to creep in over the bay. As I turned off the highway onto the county road, a pair of mallards swooped low over the bridge that crossed the slough. Squirrel hadn't been looking at the scenery. She was still thinking about our visit with Earlene.

"You know what I think, Billy? I think that J could be for Jacob. That box came from the south jetty where he was attacked."

"I've been thinking about that, too," I said. "It makes sense, in a way."

"If the J is for Jacob, then Olive must be the name of the

woman he was with that night on the beach. I wonder who she was."

"Did you notice the look on Earlene's face when she put the pendant back in the box and closed the lid?"

"What do you mean?"

"When she closed the box, she stared at the top for a second. She had a kind of frowny look on her face. I think she saw the name, and it meant something to her."

"I don't know… If that was the case, why didn't she say anything?"

"Well, she acted like she was in a rush to get to her meeting, but I'm not so sure."

"Seems like the more we learn from Earlene, the more questions we have."

I turned into our driveway and parked beside the tankhouse. We walked back to the main house and went inside to change out of our town clothes. Squirrel took the box with the pendant from her coat pocket and set it beside her purse on the kitchen table. She filled a bucket with warm water from the laundry sink to clean Flossie up before she milked her. I grabbed my old coat from the hook on the wall beside the back door, picked up the bucket, and the two of us headed out to the barn.

Squirrel was still mulling over what we'd learned. "All that stuff Earlene said about people keeping secrets—even her father, she said."

"Yeah, that surprised me, too. I wonder what Ollie could have told her about the family history." I thought about Earlene's father, trying to remember anything he said when Pepper and I visited their place. "I don't know. He wasn't one for talking, never said much when Pepper and I were there."

"I think she's probably right about people discovering

things these days—on the internet, like she said."

When we neared the barn, I stumbled a little, and water slopped over the edge of the bucket and ran down my pants leg. "Damn," I said.

Squirrel laughed. "Better let me take that. Go check on the chickens. When I'm done with the milking, I'm gonna give Emma a call. She'll want to know what Earlene had to say."

I headed over to the chicken yard, annoyed by my clumsiness as the wet pants leg turned cold in the afternoon breeze. The chickens were happily pecking away inside the fence. The Araucanas were still in the enclosure Teddy and I had made for them. Our rooster strutted nearby, casting a lecherous eye on the newcomers. He put on a show for them, fanning his wings and crowing. I figured he couldn't wait to add them to his harem.

It would be another month or so before the Araucanas were old enough to start laying, but Squirrel and I were brimming with "egg-spectation." I'd built a couple of nesting boxes, lined them with straw, and set them in the old rabbit hutch we'd refurbished. I put in a couple old golf balls as decoy eggs to let the new girls know what the boxes were for.

I filled the water pans and tossed a little extra feed nearby. The chickens rushed over to see what I'd brought, tumbling over each other to get to the treat. I didn't have to worry about them stuffing themselves, though. Chickens didn't overfeed like the large animals. That was one thing about chickens. They knew their limits.

The chickens didn't go to roost till the sun went down, so I'd have to come back later to shut them in for the night. People say that farmers go to bed with the chickens and get up with the cows. That was probably true in the old days before farms had electricity, but not so much now. Still, Squirrel and

I had Flossie to get us up in the morning, so maybe they're half right.

I closed up the gate to the chicken yard and met up with Squirrel. She was still thinking about our visit with Earlene.

"I'm gonna call Emma when we get back to the house."

"Good idea," I said. I wished she'd wait till after dinner, but I didn't say anything. I knew it wouldn't do any good.

As soon as we were in the kitchen, Squirrel grabbed the phone and dialed Emma's number. She stretched out the cord and sat down at the table. I put water in the coffee pot, scooped some grounds into the basket, and set the pot on the stove.

"Hi, Emma. How are you?" Squirrel listened for a bit, being polite I supposed, as Emma caught her up on whatever she'd been doing. Squirrel nodded, said "How interesting," and "Oh, I know." I knew how eager Squirrel was to tell Emma what we'd found out from Earlene. But when those two got to talking, I knew it would take a while, and I was hungry. Squirrel was just getting started.

I rummaged through the cupboards, looking for something I could fix for dinner. Usually Squirrel cooked dinner, but I knew my way around the kitchen. I'd been an only child, and Mom made sure I could fend for myself when I had to.

I found a couple of cans of Libby's corned beef hash in the cupboard. That was a start. I got out a cast iron skillet and set it on the stove. I opened the cans, spooned the hash into the skillet, and spread it out. I turned on the burner, and got a couple of eggs from the fridge.

While the hash was heating, I got down a couple of dinner plates and took out some lettuce and tomatoes. I pulled off some lettuce leaves, washed them, and set them on the edge of the plates. I put some tomato slices on top.

Squirrel was busy bringing Emma up to date on our visit to the cultural center. I listened with one ear while I stirred the hash. The potatoes in the hash were beginning to brown, so I pulled the skillet off the burner and put on the lid. I didn't want to put the eggs on top till Squirrel got off the phone. Timing was everything.

The coffee was perking away, bubbling up into the glass at the top. I turned the burner off and got down a couple of mugs. Squirrel was still talking with Emma, but she'd been doing more listening than talking for a while. I wondered what Emma was telling her.

"Really?" Squirrel said. "What did you find out?"

She had my attention, but there was another long pause while Squirrel listened, nodding now and then. "Too bad," she said. "That seemed like such a good idea."

I took the lid off the skillet and carefully cracked two eggs onto the hash. I put the lid on to keep the heat in so the eggs would cook, and popped a couple of slices of bread into the toaster. I knew they'd finish talking sooner or later, but I hoped it was sooner. I was really hungry.

Their conversation seemed to be winding down. The toast popped up. I buttered the slices, cut them into triangles, and set them on the edge of the plates. As I scooped the hash onto the plates, careful not to break the egg yolk, Squirrel said, "Well, you could give it a try—let us know what you find out."

They said their good-byes and Squirrel hung up the phone, sitting back down at the table. I set the dinner plates on the table and went back to the stove to pour coffee into the mugs. "So what did Emma have to say when you told her what we found out?" I took the mugs over to the table and sat down.

"Well, Emma was impressed, I think. She thought what

Earlene told us about the pendant, especially the Hupa word, was really interesting. I told her what Earlene said about the island, how the story was a lot different from what we thought. Emma said her dives into the *Herald's* archives had made her rethink a lot of what we were told, starting with the account of what happened out there on the south jetty."

Squirrel dipped a piece of toast in the egg and took a bite. "Thanks for cooking."

"I was hungry," I said.

"Me, too." She stirred some egg into the hash with her fork and took a bite. She looked at me and smiled. "This is delicious."

"Thanks. It was pretty easy."

Squirrel took a sip of coffee, swallowed. "I told her what you said about the look on Earlene's face when she put the pendant back in the box, but Emma didn't think it meant anything, thought maybe Earlene was just looking at the box itself."

"She say anything else?"

"Actually, she did. When I told her the Recorder's Office had been a dead end, she said she'd come up with another way to learn who this Jake Whitehorse fellow was."

"Really?" I said. "I thought she'd given up by now."

"Apparently not. She still wants to find out who he was. She went online, trying to find his service records, figured she'd be sure to come up with something."

"That's a great idea. Don't know why we didn't think of that sooner."

"I thought so, too," Squirrel said. "But it turned out to be another dead end—for a different reason."

"What do you mean?"

"The service records were kept in the National Personnel Records Center in St. Louis. In 1973, a fire destroyed millions of records. According to Emma, eighty percent of the Army files for soldiers discharged between 1912 and 1960 were lost."

"I don't suppose Jake's are in the twenty percent that survived?"

Squirrel frowned. "Afraid not. Emma says the Records Center has tried to reconstruct the files, but a lot are missing."

"That's too bad. Looks like we're just gonna have to give up."

"That's what I told her. But she said our visit with Earlene has given her a new idea to think about. She says she'll keep looking."

"She didn't tell you what the 'new idea' was?"

"No—just said she'd let me know if she came up with anything."

17

Teddy and Dolly showed up Saturday afternoon to tend to their animals. The senior prom had been held the night before, and both of them looked a little the worse for wear. There'd been an all-night party afterward at the home of some friends, and they'd stayed for a few hours before calling it a night.

Dolly had dark circles under her eyes, but she smiled as she told us about the fun they'd had and showed us pictures she'd taken with her phone. She was still wearing her "prom hair"—an up-do with little curls at the sides. In the pictures, she looked swell in a pretty pale blue dress, and Teddy, wearing the inevitable tux, had cleaned up well, too. They looked so grown up it was hard to remember they were the same kids I had known since they were eighth graders.

The formal photos they took at the prom would come later, and Squirrel and I made them promise to save one for us. Squirrel put her arm around me and leaned against my shoulder as we watched them, heading out, arm in arm, to take care of their animals.

"I'm sure going to miss those kids when they graduate and go off to school," Squirrel said.

"Me, too," I said.

The house phone rang, and Squirrel hurried into the kitchen to answer. It was Emma. We hadn't heard from her in a while. I wondered if she was calling to tell us what her "new idea" was all about. Squirrel listened for a long time without saying much besides "Oh?" and "Really?" and "I never thought of that." My ear hustling wasn't getting me anywhere, so I reheated my coffee in the microwave and sat out on the front porch to watch the traffic go by while I waited to hear what Emma'd had to say.

The morning overcast had burned away, and a few white clouds drifted south on a gentle breeze that overlaid the clean, salty tang of the bay with a little pulp mill flavor. Out on the road, two boys on bicycles pedaled toward the slough, fishing poles poking out past the handlebars. I remembered the days when my trusty Schwinn was my passport to the world. Now I was just an old guy sitting on the porch, watching the world go by. Squirrel didn't like it when I said things like that. It was a good thing I had her to keep me grounded.

"There you are," she said as she came out of the house. "I was looking all over for you, Billy." She sat beside me on the wicker love seat.

"I was just watching the world go by. I knew you were talking to Emma—figured it would be a while."

"You know how my sister loves to talk."

"I do. She have anything to tell us?"

"You remember she said she had a new idea to find out about that Jacob Whitehorse?"

"What was that all about?" I said.

"Emma was looking into the Indian Census Rolls. She says the federal government has collected census data on Native Americans since the late 1800s."

"Sounds like a good idea. Did she find anything?"

"Well, she was working on it, but there were some problems."

"She say what they were?"

"Of course," she said. Squirrel gave me that look. I was interrupting again.

"Sorry—go ahead." I took a sip from my coffee mug.

"Well, first of all, Emma's boss at the *Herald* has her

working on a special sesquicentennial issue, digging into the paper's archives for a two-page spread of interesting gems from Buck's Landing's history over the last hundred and fifty years."

"Wow. I knew the *Herald* had been around a long time, but a hundred and fifty years, that's really something."

"She said Horace Huddleson started the paper just a few years after Buck's Landing sprang up beside the bay. She was up to the 1970s with her earlier work, but that's on hold now. So far, she's got a biographical sketch about Whitney Buck and another about Noah Mackey."

"Nothing about their treatment of the local Indians, I bet."

"Probably not. There might be stories about the oyster pirates and the red light houses on Two Street, but the shady doings of the lumber barons who built the town will be glossed over with accounts of how they used their fortunes to build the theater and the opera house. There'll be the usual pictures of men perched on springboards felling giant redwoods with double-bitted axes and sober-faced pioneer families posed in Victorian finery."

"Still, worth a look," I said.

"Oh, it probably will be. But Emma had to stop beating the bushes to find Jacob Whitehorse."

"Checking those Indian Census Rolls sounds promising."

"Emma thinks so. She started looking, but didn't get very far. She says the Indian census rolls are online now, but most of the sites want you to subscribe before you can access the information."

"Pretty typical, these days," I said.

"Sites like Fold3, Family Search, and Ancestry are all pay sites. Emma didn't want to go there. She's pretty sure there's somewhere to get access to the census rolls without paying.

She just hasn't found it yet."

"So what's the plan?"

"Emma says we should go online ourselves, use our computer to search for the census records."

I wasn't too keen on that idea. I took another sip of coffee. It had gone cold, and I set the mug on the wicker table beside the love seat. "I bet the cultural center has access to those records. Maybe we should ask Earlene to look into it."

"I think we've pestered Earlene enough. Emma's sure we can find what we want to know if we keep looking."

"Okay, but I'm pretty sure Earlene knows more. You saw the look on her face when she saw the name on the lid of the box. She hasn't told us everything she knows."

"Maybe you're right. But let's see what we can find first. Earlene said that word on the pendant was a Hupa word. When we get access to the census rolls, we'll start looking at the Hupa records. We can always ask Earlene later."

"If those records go back to the 1800s, it could take a while."

"If Jacob was in his twenties when he was attacked on the beach, he was probably born in the early 1920s, so that should make it easier."

"If you say so," I said. Emma's determination seemed to have rubbed off on Squirrel. I was curious, too, but Squirrel sounded genuinely excited. I hoped she'd find something, but I wasn't going to hold my breath.

Teddy and Dolly stopped to say good-bye as we walked out to the barn to tend to the afternoon chores. They were looking a little perkier than they had earlier.

"How're the beasts coming along?" I asked.

"My lamb is looking good," Dolly said. "She's gaining weight like she should be, I think."

"Charlie's coming along, too," Teddy said. "He leads pretty well now, getting used to placing his feet like he's supposed to."

Squirrel smiled. "Didn't step on any toes this time?"

"I watched where he was stepping," Dolly said. "Can't say as much for Teddy at the prom."

Teddy looked embarrassed, blushing and shuffling his feet. "I told you I didn't know much about dancing."

Dolly smiled, patting Teddy on the arm. She looked at Squirrel. "Two left feet, like they say, but he's coming along, just like Charlie. We just need to practice a little more."

They got into the Scout and drove off.

"Maybe Dolly should get one of those sticks with the hook," I said.

Squirrel gave me a withering look. "Not funny," she said.

"I know. I just couldn't help myself. It was the first thing that popped into my mind."

"Seriously, we should be thinking about a graduation present for those two. Something to let them know how much we appreciate all they've done, helping us out and working with the other kids."

"That's a good idea. We'll have to give it some thought."

When Squirrel said, "We could start with a graduation party," I could see the wheels turning.

Squirrel's dive into the Indian census rolls was going to have to wait till Monday. The parents of the younger kids would be driving them out tomorrow to look over their projects and take care of their animals. Teddy and Dolly would be catching up on their sleep, and Squirrel and I would be busy all day. Squirrel needed to check the junior members' record books, and it would take both of us to keep an eye on them when they were in the garden and with the animals.

We didn't want a repeat of Dolly's mishap.

Carla Spencer would want to help me with the Araucanas. She was quite taken with "them ugly birds," as Bobby Cantwell called them. I'd have to keep an eye on that boy. Without Dolly there to moon over, Bobby might get bored and dream up some creative mischief.

I knew Squirrel couldn't wait to take up where Emma'd left off on her internet search. I was just hoping to stay out of the way.

18

After the morning chores, Squirrel and I returned to the kitchen for a leisurely breakfast. I put on the coffee while she got down the Bisquick and whipped up some batter for pancakes in the yellow Pyrex bowl her mother had used when she and Emma were kids. Squirrel loves that bowl. I never use it. I'm afraid something might happen to it, and I'd be in the doghouse for sure.

I set the cast iron skillet on the stove—little risk of damaging that—and poured in a little Wesson Oil. I turned on the burner and watched the oil spread in the skillet, tipping it to coat the bottom evenly. When the oil began to shimmer, Squirrel took over with the pancakes while I poured the coffee. She spooned in some batter for the "test" pancake that would tell if the pan was hot enough and soak up the unnecessary oil.

I sat at the table, sipping my coffee as I watched her at the stove. She tossed that first hotcake into the trash, and there was a satisfying sizzle as she spooned some more batter into the skillet. "I want to get started on that internet search," she said. "Emma thinks we might find Jacob in the Indian census rolls, but I got the idea it wasn't that easy."

Apparently Squirrel and her sister were on a first-name basis with Mr. Whitehorse now.

"How hard can it be? Can't you just google it, or something?"

"We'll see," she said. She slid the spatula under the pancake and flipped it. It hissed when it hit the pan. She turned to face me, spatula in hand. "Emma hadn't gotten very far before she had to start working on the project for the *Herald*."

"That's what you said. But still, it looks like that census business might be a good place to look. I didn't even know there was such a thing."

"Neither did I." She turned back to the stove, scooped the pancake from the skillet, and slid it onto a plate. She spooned some more batter into the pan and brought the plate over to the table. "Here you go," she said. "After breakfast, I'm going to get on the computer and see what I can find."

Squirrel seemed determined to take up the search where Emma had left off. She and Emma might be happy spending the day sitting at a computer, but I'd rather be outdoors. I hoped Squirrel would find out something. I was curious about Jacob, too.

I puttered around the yard for a few hours, finding little things to do. The 4-H kids had weeded the garden and made sure their animals were taken care of, so I had some time to myself. It was a sunny morning, but still cool as I strolled through the orchard, admiring the developing apples. Hopefully the coddling moths would leave us alone this year.

I leaned against the fence outside the cowshed and watched Flossie crop some tasty morsels in the pasture. She raised her head to look at me, chewing contentedly, but she didn't seem interested in conversation. She flicked her tail at some flies on her back, and lowered her head, plucking another mouthful of grass.

If what Emma said was true, Squirrel's internet search was going to take a while. She wouldn't want me looking over her shoulder. I figured I'd give her some time, and see what she came up with.

I strolled over to see what the chickens were doing. I filled the water pans and tossed a little scratch around so I could watch them tumble over each other to get to the treat. Our rooster still had his eye on the Araucanas, fanning his wings and doing his little happy dance to show off for them. I hated to turn the new girls out with that guy in the yard. We'd have to look out for them. Roosters are not gentle lovers.

When I couldn't come up with anything to do that couldn't be put off for a while, I walked back to the house to see if Squirrel had found anything. It was nearing lunchtime, and I figured that was as good an excuse as any. I could rustle up something to eat and check on her at the same time.

When there was no sign of her in the kitchen, I knew Squirrel was still upstairs searching online for the Indian census rolls. Emma had set up our computer in Squirrel's old room, clearing everything off the dressing table, except for Squirrel's pink princess phone, which was still connected to our landline.

I'm sure lots of kids have computers in their rooms now, but the computer looked out of place amid the treasures from Squirrel's growing up years. She had the usual collection of stuffed animals and a few American Girl and Madame Alexander dolls, but a lot of the things she'd kept were from her 4-H activities—ribbons from the county fair, sashes and pins, plaques and trophies, and a lot of photos of her standing beside one animal or another holding an award of some kind. There'd been no need to put away her things from the past to make room for the child we never had.

I put together a couple of tuna sandwiches, set them on a plate with some apple slices, and headed upstairs to see how she was doing.

"I made some lunch," I said as I entered the room. Squirrel was hunched over, looking at something on the computer screen. I set the plate on the edge of the dressing table. Squirrel looked at what I'd brought, grabbed an apple slice, and looked up at me.

She nibbled at the slice and pointed at the screen with the remainder. "This is turning out to be a lot harder than you'd expect." She looked at me and smiled. "Thanks for making lunch. I needed a break."

"Find anything out yet?"

"Not exactly." She snagged another slice and took a bite. "Emma was right. If you google "Indian census roll," all kinds of sites come up, but they're all pay sites. The census records come from the National Archives, but if you go there, they refer you to their "partners," sites like Ancestry and Family Search. And those sites all want you to subscribe in order to access the census records."

"The National Archives sold the records to those other companies. It's all about money now—even with the government."

"Yeah," she said. "I thought we were stuck, but I remembered that Emma said there'd be a free site somewhere, so I kept looking till I found something."

"Did you get into the census rolls?"

"Sort of…" She looked at the sandwiches I'd brought up. "Let's eat first. Then I'll show you what I found."

I wanted to see what she'd come up with, but it sounded like that was going to take a while, so I picked up half a sandwich and dug in.

I liked being in Squirrel's room. The window was open a few inches, and a soft breeze ruffled the lacy curtains. I imagined her as a teenager sitting at the dressing table in the morning, brushing her hair and tying it in a ponytail as she got ready for school. When I looked at her now, sandwich in hand, I could still see the red-haired girl with the dazzling blue eyes that boarded the school bus in the morning and again felt the little shiver that went through me as she made her way down the aisle to sit next to me.

When we had finished our lunch, Squirrel showed me what she'd found. She tapped a key to wake up the computer, and a screen appeared, filled with black squares labeled "NATIONAL ARCHIVES MICROFILM PUBLICATIONS" in bold white letters. There were dozens of them. Below each black square was a white square labeled "Indian census rolls, 1885-1940 (microform)."

"Wow," I said. "What, exactly, are we looking at?"

"Each one of those is apparently a roll of microfilm from the Indian census."

"They all look the same."

"Yeah, but look what happens when I click on one of them." She moved the cursor over one of the squares and clicked the mouse. "NATIONAL ARCHIVES MICROFILM PUBLICATIONS" appeared again on the screen. At the bottom of the page, it said "(1 0f 802)."

Squirrel clicked on one of the arrows at the bottom of the screen and the display turned to another page that said "Microcopy 595, Roll 494." To the right of that was a page with the seal of the National Archives that said "Shawnee, 1932-1933." A few more clicks showed the census information typed in on ledger pages.

"They're all like this," she said. "You can't tell what's on the roll till you open it up. They're not even in any order." She clicked on another one. "This is Roll 21 from 1937."

She went back, clicked on a different one. "This is Roll 35. It's from 1901."

"There's no index?"

"Not that I can see. It's gonna take forever if I have to open each of these till I find the Hupa records—and find the right years, too."

I mulled it over for a moment. "Do you think the pay sites

would have indexed the records?"

"I thought of that, too," Squirrel said. "I called Emma to ask her what she thought. After all, she'd been doing the same thing, digitizing the *Herald's* microfilm records."

I recalled that machine in her office and all those rolls of microfilm. "What did she have to say?"

"When I told her what I'd found, she was appalled, said this was sloppy work. She had organized the paper's back issues, put them in order, and provided an index so people could find what they were looking for."

"What did she think about looking on the pay sites?" I asked.

"She said organizing the hundreds of census rolls would be an enormous job. It would cost the pay sites too much to do all that work. They might have done something, but she doubts it." She turned toward me, frowning. "I think we're stuck with what we're looking at now."

I saw the frustration in her face. "I guess we'll just have to keep looking." I chuckled, remembering a joke Pepper once told me. "Do you remember what the plow said to the tractor?"

Squirrel looked at me blankly for a moment. "No—what?"

I tried to put a little husky tone in my voice. "A little deeper, John Deere."

"That's terrible," she said.

"Pepper told me that one when we were teenagers."

"Sounds like something Pepper would say."

"Yeah—a ghost from the past, just like Jacob. We'll probably never find out what happened to Pepper, but you might have better luck with Jacob. Just have to "dig a little deeper."

Squirrel smiled when I said that. Then she punched me in the shoulder. "We'll see, all right."

19

With all the things we had to do to keep the farm running, Squirrel's search kept getting interrupted. We were up early as usual, milking the cow, feeding the chickens and turning them out in the yard, but after breakfast, Squirrel was back in her room, going through the census rolls, one at a time, searching for the Hupa records. The evening chores were all mine.

I tried to imagine what Squirrel would find as I sat down to milk Flossie one evening. With all those rolls, would she ever find the right one? Is Jacob on any of the rolls ? The Hupa word on the pendant was a clue, but maybe it didn't mean what we thought. Maybe he came from some other part of the country.

Flossie turned her head, giving me a brown-eyed stare that said, "You again?" and plucked another mouthful of hay from the trough as I leaned my forehead against her flank. The milk pinged into the empty pail at first, changing to a comforting swish-swish as I found my rhythm and the pail began to fill. Both of us relaxed a bit. I don't know what Flossie was thinking, but my thoughts drifted through the events of the last few months since I discovered that little silver box on the beach.

Opening that box had led us to a mystery we weren't yet able to solve, but we'd come a long way. Emma's discovery of the stories in the *Herald* had put us on the right track. Karl Vogel had pushed the search along a little further when he found his grandfather's original invoice for the pendant, and Earlene had really whetted our curiosity when she explained the meaning of the Hupa word. We seemed to be stalled again, but Squirrel was determined to keep searching. I hoped she'd find some answers.

Penny, the little banty hen, appeared in the doorway as I was finishing up. She clucked a few times, casting a sideways glance at me. I squirted some milk in the pan we kept for her and set it off to the side so she could have her treat. I emptied the pail into the big galvanized milk can, put the lid on tight, and lugged it over to the fridge. When I released the latch on the stanchion, Flossie backed her head out and clumped across the floor, headed back out to the pasture.

While I was cleaning things and putting them away, I heard a car pull up in the driveway. I walked out through the barn to see Teddy drive up in his Scout. Teddy always came out in the morning, never in the evening. And he always brought Dolly with him. Those two were joined at the hip. I couldn't think of one of them without thinking of the other, but Teddy was alone. Something was up, for sure.

He got out of his truck, slammed the door shut, and headed out to the pasture. I don't think he even noticed me standing in the doorway. He didn't look around, just stomped out to the field where Charlie was plucking some green shoots that had sprung up beside the watering trough next to the fence. The steer looked up, watching Teddy as he came toward him. One of the lambs grazing in the field on the other side of the fence knew something was off, too. She threw her head up, then went stiff-legged, and bolted away to join the others further out in the field.

I walked around the corner of the barn to see what was going on. Teddy stroked Charlie's neck a few times, then sat on the edge of the trough. He pulled an apple from his pocket and tossed it on the ground for Charlie, who immediately snatched it up and crunched it. The two of them looked at each other for a while. I thought Charlie was hoping for another apple. I didn't know what Teddy was hoping for. I decided to see what was going on.

I opened the gate and headed into the pasture. Charlie looked my way as I crossed the field. Teddy turned to see what he was looking at. The two of them watched me as I came toward them.

"Hey, Teddy, what's up?" I said.

Teddy looked my way, then glanced over at the big steer. "Not much, I guess. I just came out to see how Charlie was getting along."

Charlie apparently gave up hope of a second apple and stepped away. He put his head down and cropped at the grass.

"Charlie's fine." I paused for a second, changing the subject. "How are you?"

When Teddy didn't say anything right away, I asked, "Where's Dolly?"

Teddy looked at me then. His eyes were puffy. He looked miserable. "We had a fight."

I joined Teddy, sitting beside him on the edge of the trough. "I'm surprised," I finally said. "You always get along so well. What was the fight about?"

"Dolly got accepted at the veterinary school in Davis."

"That's great news. Aren't you happy for her?"

"I suppose. She wants to be a vet like her old man, but if she goes away to school, she might not come back."

I didn't know what to say. It was a long time since I was Teddy's age, but I could see the pain in his eyes. "She'll be home for holidays and probably in the summer. It's not the end of the world."

"That's what she said, but I'm not so sure. There's lots of guys better lookin' than me."

"It's not about looks, Teddy. Good looks wear off, but what's in your heart—that's what counts."

Teddy nodded, looking down at the ground. "I suppose," he said again. "But I don't know. How does anyone know what's in someone's heart?"

That was a big question, for sure. I was getting out of my depth.

"You're still getting to know each other, discovering who you are. It takes time. You'll work things out." I almost said, "one way or the other," but held my tongue at the last moment.

"Maybe—I hope so."

Teddy still looked like a boy whose puppy'd just gotten run over. I tried to change the subject.

"So what are your plans when school is out?"

"I can't afford to go away to school. I got into Buck's. I can live at home and commute to school."

Whitney Buck State College was just across the bay, north of the Landing and named for the founder, but all the locals just called it Buck's. It was a small school, not much for liberal arts, but a good place for forestry and wildlife students.

"Know what you want to major in?" I asked.

"Not really. Figure I'll just start out and see where it leads. Might want to be a game warden, something outdoors like that."

"Sounds like a plan. You and Dolly both love animals." I paused, trying to find something comforting to say. "Take your time, see how things work out, find out what you want to do."

"I suppose." He looked at Charlie for a moment, then turned back toward me. "Dolly'll be fishing in a bigger pond, y'know? I can just see her falling for some good-looking guy in a white lab coat."

Squirrel had already cooked dinner by the time I got back

to the house. She was excited about something she'd found on the internet. When I told her about the trouble between Teddy and Dolly, it toned down her enthusiasm a little, but she promised to show me after dinner. I could tell she was excited. "I found him, Billy," was all she would tell me.

We worked our way through Squirrel's meatloaf-and-baked-potato meal while we sympathized with Teddy's plight and his worries about losing Dolly when she leaves Buck's Landing to go to school.

"They're only high school kids, Billy," Squirrel said.

"We were only high school kids, too," I said.

Squirrel looked at me and smiled. "Well, it will happen if it's meant to—look at us."

"Indeed," was all I could manage to say.

After dinner, we went upstairs so Squirrel could show me what she'd found. She booted up the computer and brought up the site she'd bookmarked. Sitting beside her, I looked at the screen and saw the now familiar NATIONAL ARCHIVES MICROFILM PUBLICATIONS on the first page. She clicked on the arrow at the bottom, and the next page said MICROCOPY 595 and ROLL 184 below that. On the facing page it said:

> Roll 184
> Hoopa Valley (Hupa or Hoopa),
> Klamath,
> and other Indians)
> 1923-1929

First there were a dozen pages for Smith River Indians, followed by eleven for the Indians of the Lower Klamath. After that came seventeen pages for Klamath River Indians.

Fifteen pages after that were devoted to "Hoopa Indians of the Hoopa Valley"—Finally!

"I had no idea there were so many tribes," I said.

"There are more on this roll. Bear River, Blue Lake, and Eel River Indians were all part of the Hoopa Valley Agency."

"Didn't you just show me the Hupa census?"

"Yes, but he wasn't listed in that one. I figured if he was old enough to serve in the war, he was probably born in the 1920s. That census was for 1923."

"You did find his name, right?"

"Be patient. I was just showing you what I went through. The pages on this roll have everything up to 1929. I only had to get to 1924."

She flipped through to the census for 1924. The information was typewritten on ruled ledger sheets, including the date the census was taken and the name of the agent who conducted it. There were columns for the person's "Indian name, English name, Relationship, and Date of Birth." The names were listed alphabetically, last name first. There were no names in the column for "Indian Name." That struck me as odd.

"Why don't they list the Indian names?" I asked.

"These are standard forms they used for years, apparently. The really old rolls showed the Indian names, but by the turn of the century most everyone seems to have taken English names and that column is usually blank."

"Explains a lot, in a way," I said. "More of that 'vanishing Indian' stuff Earlene was talking about."

"It's too bad. The old names had a lot of character. I looked at some of them." Squirrel looked at me and smiled. "There was one fellow called Peter Pretty Bear. I liked that one."

"Probably a translation from the Native language."

"Yeah—another thing that's been lost."

Squirrel turned back to the computer and flipped through some more pages till she found what she was looking for. "Here," she said. "Look at this."

She moved the cursor to show me: "Whitehorse, George, Hus, 1885." Below that was "Minnie, Wife, 1889." Finally, under that, was "Jacob, son, 2/14/24."

"Most dates of birth just give the year, but Jacob was only a few months old when the census was taken, so they have the exact date. There were some other entries like that."

"Well," I said, "it looks like you found him all right."

Squirrel gave me a sad smile, "It took a lot of searching, but I didn't really find out anything that would solve the mystery. We know he was Hupa, like the word on the pendant suggested, but that doesn't really help us."

"According to that," I said, pointing to the screen, "he was born on Valentine's Day."

"Again, interesting, but not really helpful."

I knew Squirrel was disappointed. So was I. She had found what she was looking for, but had hoped for more.

I rested my hand on top of hers and gave it a little squeeze. "We'll just have to keep looking. Jacob may be lost forever, like Pepper, but maybe not. We just need to look in the right place."

20

Squirrel was pretty discouraged. All that searching hadn't told us much more than we already suspected. We'd been right about the Hupa connection, but confirming that didn't really help. The birthdate was the only thing new to go on. We mulled that one over at the breakfast table the next morning.

"Emma couldn't find Jacob in the obituaries," Squirrel said. "Do you think he could still be alive, Billy?"

I thought about it, stirring my oatmeal around the bowl with the spoon. "If he was born in '24, he'd have been twenty-one at the end of the war." I was doing the math in my head, but Squirrel beat me to the answer.

"If he was twenty-one in 1945, he'd be eighty-four now."

"Well, I suppose he could still be alive. Emma couldn't find him in any of her usual sources. Maybe he just moved away."

"I spent all that time searching those census rolls. I don't know what I was expecting to find."

I hadn't been the one hunched over the computer, but I knew how frustrated she felt. "Maybe it wasn't a total waste," I said. "It adds a little to what we already knew."

"Nothing really useful, as far as I can tell," she said. Squirrel pushed back her chair, gathered up her breakfast dishes, and set them in the sink. She turned to look at me, leaning back against the drainboard. "I think I'm giving up. We're just chasing the wind. It was a longshot from the start. We've got lots of other things to think about."

"I was hoping for more, too. But I think you're right." I walked across the kitchen, set my bowl in the sink, and put my arms around her. "Who knows?" I said, "Something might yet turn up."

"Maybe. But I'm not gonna lose any more sleep over it."

We muddled along for a couple of weeks, our mystery set aside like the silver box on the mantel. It caught my eye from time to time, but we had other things to tend to.

Teddy and Dolly had invited us to their graduation, showing up at the farm with coveted guest tickets for the ceremony. The high school in Buck's Landing served students from the town as well as the surrounding areas, eighteen hundred kids in all. There were five hundred and ten in the senior class, so guests at the afternoon graduation were limited.

Carefully laid out rows of folding chairs on the floor of the gym barely accommodated the graduating seniors. Family and other guests were relegated to the bleachers and the balcony above them on each side. The situation was enough to give the fire marshal fits, but school security officers kept the aisles open and made sure the guests behaved themselves.

It was hot up in the balcony where Squirrel and I sat. People fanned themselves with their programs as they chattered excitedly. When the graduates filed in to the familiar phrases of "Pomp and Circumstance," grinning parents strained to pick out their kids on the crowded gym floor.

The graduates were seated alphabetically. It took Squirrel and me a few moments to spot Teddy and Dolly, who were seated apart. Dolly's last name, Aguirre, put her near the front. Teddy's last name was Mercer, putting him squarely in the middle.

Katie Iverson, the valedictorian, made a fine speech filled with typical youthful optimism about the promising outlook for the class of 2008. Katie had been one of my students in junior high, a bright girl who was a delight in class. As she talked about the great things that lay ahead, I thought about our own graduation, when Squirrel and I had sat in those uncomfortable chairs on the gym floor, listening to a similar speech by one of our classmates.

Mickey Madsen had quoted Thoreau, telling us "if you have built castles in the air, your work need not be lost; that is where they should be. Now put the foundations under them." It sounded good at the time—uplifting and inspirational. All we had to do was put in a little work to reach our dreams.

My optimism has taken a few hits over the years. I believed all that stuff once, but I know fate and circumstance step in to trample the dreams of youth. Nobody's future is guaranteed. As I listened to Katie, I thought about Earlene and Pepper and how things had turned out for them. I was reminded how lucky Squirrel and I had been.

One of the grads near the back of the gym pulled an inflatable beach balloon from under his robe, blew it up, and batted it over the heads of the others. It sailed toward the stage, batted along by whoever it landed on. The lighthearted prank jolted me from my gloomy reverie, as I watched the ball bounce from one grad to another. The red-white-and-yellow balloon had almost made it to the stage when it was finally captured by one of the security officers who stabbed it and tossed it in a trash can while the kids booed. Katie soldiered on with her optimistic speech, though the balloon incident took some of the air out of her closing remarks.

Darren Farnsworth, the school superintendent, made a droning speech so boring that it launched two more beach balls. He gave the grads a stony look before he settled down to introduce the graduating class and turn over the handing out of diplomas to two of the school counselors, who took turns reading the graduates' names.

Everyone cheered as the kids trooped across the stage when their names were called. They traded handshakes for diplomas, smiling and waving as they descended the steps on the other side and returned to their seats.

Squirrel and I cheered for Dolly and Teddy when their turns came, feeling as proud as parents. We had watched them grow over the years and knew they had turned out fine.

When the last name was called and an impatient-looking Tony Zimmerman finally crossed the stage, the principal, Madeline Quinn, made a few congratulatory remarks before the graduates tossed their caps in the air and filed out into the parking lot to rejoin their families.

When we caught up with them, Teddy and Dolly had found each other and were standing together with their parents. Everyone was all smiles. Lorna Aguirre was a little distant, but Dolly's father seemed happy to see us. We congratulated the kids, and Squirrel snapped pictures of them holding their diplomas. Then she got Teddy's father to take one of us with the two of them.

When we were preparing to leave, Teddy's father thanked us for our work with the 4-H, and we told him what a help Teddy was. Dolly hugged each of us in turn, and there were handshakes all around. They weren't our children, but it was a precious moment nevertheless, and we were happy they'd made us a part of it.

I'm not the only one who occasionally needs to "get out and blow the stink off," as Squirrel likes to say when I'm getting antsy about something. The unproductive internet search had left her down in the dumps. We'd stopped talking about it, but I could tell that the disappointment was still nagging at her. When I noticed her staring off into space from time to time, I knew what she was thinking about.

When I get like that, I need to go off and be by myself for a bit, somewhere outdoors away from other people. I was an only child and being alone for a time doesn't bother me. I'm better company afterward, I'm sure. Squirrel has told me as much.

Squirrel prefers to head to town, maybe do a little recreational shopping, meet up with a friend, things like that. At breakfast one morning, a few days after the graduation, I was treated to that vacant stare again.

"Why don't you give Emma a call," I said. "See what she's been up to lately. Maybe the two of you could get together."

She turned to look at me, my words finally sinking in. "Maybe I will. It would be nice to get away for a while."

Squirrel called her sister a little later in the morning and asked her if she had time to go out to lunch. As luck would have it, Emma had finished her project for the special edition of the *Herald* and was delighted with the prospect of getting out of the office for a couple of hours.

Squirrel set up the ironing board and put together a spiffy outfit of navy slacks and a crisp white blouse. Emma wasn't likely to suggest lunch at some fast food emporium. She and Frank avoided the huddled masses whenever possible. Squirrel wanted to be ready for whatever fancy spot Emma had in mind.

When she was ready, Squirrel grabbed her coat, gave me a peck on the cheek, and headed out the back door. "I should be back in time to take care of Flossie."

"Don't worry," I said. "She and I are still on speaking terms. Have a good time." I knew when those two got together, it would be a while. Just like their conversations on the phone, Emma would do most of the talking. But Squirrel would enjoy herself. She needed a break.

The morning overcast had cleared, and a light breeze had come up. The windmill turned lazily overhead as I walked past the tankhouse on my way to the orchard.

The apples were coming on now, still green but growing in size. I hoped the spraying had kept the coddling moths at bay. I didn't see any sign of them yet, but they could be persistent.

Russell Posey had planted several apple varieties, mostly Rome Beauty, Gravenstein, and Golden Delicious, but there were a few heirloom trees in our orchard, too. I liked them because they were different. They had interesting names, like Red Astrachan and Northern Spy, names you never saw on the grocery store shelf.

One of my favorites was the little variety called Red June. As its name suggests, it ripens early. The apples are smaller than most other varieties, but make up for their size by their juicy flavor. The apples on that tree had good color now, but they didn't look quite ready to me. I plucked one off to check. It didn't come off easily, another sign they weren't really ripe. I cut the apple open to look at the seeds. They were just starting to turn brown, but were mostly white. It would be a few more weeks before they were ripe enough. I took a bite anyway, but my mouth puckered up, and I spit it out. I needed to wait a little longer.

The Red June is prone to apple scab, a fungus that can spoil the fruit. It shows up early on the new leaves, but I didn't see any damage so far. The fungus could overwinter in dead leaves and fruit left on the ground, but we'd been careful to clear that stuff away.

From the orchard, I went to the barnyard to check up on the chickens. Squirrel'd been busy getting ready for her date with Emma and hadn't had time to do anything other than to let them out in the yard. I told her not to worry—I'd see to it.

I tossed out some scratch to give the hens something to do while I took a look in the henhouse. Penny, the banty hen, followed me inside. She strutted around, clucking at me while I checked the nesting boxes for eggs. I figured she was looking forward to her treat, hoping it was milking time. "You'll have to wait," I told her. She tipped her head, looking at me with one eye, and went back outside.

The hens had been busy overnight, and I gathered up half a dozen eggs from the nesting boxes. I crossed the yard to check on the Araucanas, keeping an eye out for the rooster. I didn't trust that guy. He usually didn't bother me, but he came after Bobby Cantwell one day, sinking his spurs in Bobby's leg, and pecking him like crazy. The poor kid was afraid to go in the chicken yard after that. Once, when he didn't think I was looking, I saw Bobby smack the fence wire with a stick and stick his tongue out at his tormentor.

I opened the gate to the Araucanas' enclosure, and went inside. I tossed out some scratch, and they went after it as soon as it hit the ground. While they were happily pecking away, I checked the nesting boxes in their coop. I was delighted to find two blue eggs among the decoys I'd put in there earlier. I couldn't wait to show them to Squirrel. I knew she'd be "egg-cited."

Squirrel pulled into the driveway around four-thirty. When she came into the kitchen through the back door, she had a newspaper tucked under her arm and a big smile on her face. I could tell the trip to town had lifted her spirits. I'd put the blue eggs in a little bowl on the table, and she spotted them right away. She set down her purse, laid the newspaper beside it, and picked up the bowl.

"The new girls left us a present," I said.

"I see." She picked one of the eggs up and inspected it.

"It's a little earlier than we expected, but that's good. They might turn out to be good producers."

"Looks like it. Long as they don't get egg-bound or beat up by that rooster. We'll need to feed 'em right. I'll add some layer ration and calcium to their feed."

"They should be fine," she said. She put the egg back in the bowl and turned to leave the room. "I'm gonna change out of these clothes and go tend to Flossie."

"What did Emma have to say?"

Squirrel took a few steps, then turned back. "I'll tell you about it later. She gave us a copy of the *Herald's* special edition. She seemed really pleased with how it came out. That's it on the table. We were so busy catching up on things, I didn't get a chance to look at it."

Squirrel grabbed her purse and headed into the bedroom to change. While she was gone, I rinsed the coffee pot, filled it with water, and scooped some fresh coffee into the basket. As I set the pot on the stove, Squirrel passed through the kitchen on her way to the barn.

"Give my regards to Flossie," I said as she left.

I sat at the table and picked up the newspaper to take a look. An article on the front page described a labor dispute involving workers and management at the pulp mill across the bay. The first copy of the *Herald* Emma had shown us, the one with the brief article about the incident on the south jetty, had a nearly identical headline on its front page—a different mill back then, but the same struggle between the workers and their bosses. Some things never change.

I worked my way through the paper as the coffee pot burbled on the stove, the pleasant aroma drifting across the room. I'd just gotten to Emma's two-page spread when the coffee was done. I poured myself a cup and returned to the table to see what she'd come up with.

The article recounted important events in the history of Buck's Landing and provided a look at the people who created them, beginning with the arrival of Whitney Buck in 1854. I sipped at my too-hot coffee, making my way through the sections. By the time it was cool enough to drink, something had caught my eye. I forgot about the coffee and stared at the page. I was still turning an idea over in my mind when Squirrel returned from the barn.

21

Emma had done herself proud, crowding 150 years of Buck's Landing history into two pages and making it attractive and interesting at the same time. Excerpts from the *Herald's* archives told of past events, beginning with a sketch about Whitney Buck's arrival on Heron Bay in 1854 and the creation of the redwood mill that made his fortune. A photo of the man, one of those somber pioneer portraits, accompanied the article. He had an Abe Lincoln beard, one of those chin curtains without the moustache, and a piercing stare that made me think he must have been a shrewd guy, the kind you didn't want to mess with.

A series of articles dredged from the archives told of the Landing's raucous beginnings. Fisheries sprang up on the bay as other settlers arrived, seeking their fortunes in different enterprises. Along with them came the usual assortment of roughnecks and bully boys who frequented the saloons, gambling dens, and red light houses that blossomed on Two Street and gave it its scandalous reputation.

In the 1880s local businessmen led by Whitney Buck organized an effort to build rail lines to ship their products more reliably than the lumber schooners then in use, but their efforts failed. Many years would pass before that would happen. Meanwhile, oyster pirates raided beds in the tidal flats on the eastern side of the bay, sneaking in by night and sailing out before dawn, headed toward San Francisco markets.

The Indians who inhabited Heron Bay and the surrounding area long before the white settlers arrived got short shrift in the excerpts from the *Herald's* archives. More modern events like the renovation of the Mackey Building, home to the cultural center, were given a couple of column inches near the end.

A long piece on Noah Mackey highlighted his contributions to the town. He had come along almost fifty years after Buck sailed into the harbor, but he had made his own timber fortune following in the founder's footsteps. The article described how he built his mansion on Mackey island after the "removal" of the Indians and went on to tell about construction of the opera house and the theater he built upstairs in the building he named for himself.

In 1920 Noah married Amelia Cooper, the daughter of Judge Langston Cooper, who'd laid out half the town lots in the early days of Buck's Landing, acquiring his own fortune. The couple moved into the big house on the island. Amelia died young, leaving Mackey to raise their daughter, with the help of an Indian housekeeper.

Mackey was an avid fisherman and a frequent visitor to the Klamath River in salmon season until his death in 1950. The article said he was "devoted" to his daughter, always taking her with him on his fishing trips and whenever he was away on business. I remembered what Earlene had told us, how that "devotion" was something else, a smothering that drove her out of the house after Mackey died.

A picture included with the piece showed Mackey on one of his fishing trips. He was standing with his daughter and an Indian fishing guide in front of a small boat. He wore one of those big walrus moustaches under a broad-brimmed hat and was holding up a large salmon with his right hand, his left arm resting on his teen-aged daughter's shoulder. His fingers were hooked into the gills, the salmon hanging nearly to the ground. A couple of fishing rods were leaned up against the boat. A handwritten date on the photo said "on the river, September 1938."

Other items Emma had dredged from the *Herald's* archives described the 1956 earthquake that damaged the old courthouse built in the 1880s. Another quake in 1964 opened cracks in pavements downtown and shattered storefront windows. A flood later that year washed out highway bridges and destroyed the rail lines that had finally been built to haul timber to San Francisco Bay. The diesel trucks that still rumble through town every day took up the slack, and the lines were never rebuilt.

The later articles highlighted the renovation of the Landing's waterfront, creating the quaint "old town" that replaced the rough and tumble Two Street saloons and dilapidated warehouses with the upscale shops and trendy eateries that are so popular now. The article included before and after pictures of the grand theater in the Mackey building, now restored as the Herron Bay Cultural Center.

My coffee had gone cold while I was reading the paper. I was still sitting at the table, thinking about the thing that had caught my eye, when Squirrel came in the back door. I heard her set the milk pail in the laundry sink and turn on the faucet. I got up to reheat my coffee in the microwave while she finished cleaning up.

When she came in, she gave me a hug, glancing at the paper spread out on the table.

"What did you think of Emma's article?" she asked. She got a cup from the cabinet, felt the coffee pot, and frowned when she realized the coffee was cold. She poured herself a cup, and I moved aside so she could get to the microwave.

"She did a great job," I said. "Take a look for yourself, see what you think. Some parts I thought were really interesting."

I wanted to see if Squirrel would notice what I had. She carried her cup to the table, spooned in some sugar, and stirred it around, the spoon rattling against the side. I watched impatiently as she sat down to read.

I knew it would take her a while. I took my coffee cup to the sink and looked out the window. Outside, the sun was sinking lower, a pinkish glow spreading across the sky to the west. A few cars rolled past on the county road. A pair of mallards winged their way toward the slough, silhouetted against the sky.

"It's a nice article," Squirrel finally said. "Lots of interesting bits from the history of the Landing."

I turned away from the window. Squirrel was shaking out the pages, folding up the paper.

"I thought so, too," I said. "Not much about the local Indians, though."

"Yeah, that bit about the removal of the Indians—massacre would've been a better word." She thought about it for a moment. "Sanitized for public consumption, probably. Imagine what Earlene would have said about it."

"Like she said, it depends on who's writing the history. Emma was just working with pieces from the paper's archives. I doubt if the reporters worried much about the local Natives back then."

Both of us had read the same stories. Like me, Squirrel had picked up on how the paper glossed over the massacre on Mackey Island. I wondered what else had caught her eye.

"See anything else in Emma's piece?" I asked.

"I remember those earthquakes and the '64 flood. The creek overflowed and our house was surrounded by water for days—had to slog through it just to get to the barn. Afterward I went with my dad to help him shovel mud out of a friend's house. What a mess that was!"

"Yeah," I said. "I remember that, too. We didn't get flooded out, but we ran out of water in the tank, and had to pump muddy water, just to flush the toilet."

Squirrel hadn't noticed what I had. I couldn't wait any longer. "Spread the paper out again," I said. "I want to show you something."

She gave me a puzzled look, then unfolded the paper on the table. I walked over to show her what I'd seen.

"Look at this picture," I said, pointing to the photo of Noah Mackey on the river.

Squirrel studied it for a moment, then looked up at me. "Okay—Mackey liked to fish. He's standing there, bragging about the big fish he's got. So what's the big deal?"

"Look at the way he's standing there. He's got the fish hooked by the gills. The other hand's on the girl's shoulder. Looks like he's got a grip on her, too. Like maybe she doesn't want to be in the picture."

Squirrel pored over the photo again. "I don't know. The picture's pretty grainy. It's hard to tell what's going on. I think you're reading a lot into it."

"Maybe so—maybe not."

"Well Earlene told us how protective he was of his daughter. Took her everywhere he went, she said."

"I remember," I said. "How old do you think she is in that picture?"

Squirrel took another look. "Probably fifteen or sixteen, maybe. So what?"

"I think kids that age, especially girls, wouldn't want to hang out with their dads, especially on a fishing trip."

"I don't know about that," she said. "I loved to hang out with my dad, help out with the animals. We had a lot of good times together."

"I know, but your dad wasn't a self-absorbed fat cat with a timber fortune and a mansion on an island in the bay. Mackey was a legend in his own mind, put his name on everything he touched."

"Still…"

"Earlene said the daughter couldn't wait to get out from under her old man's thumb. Let the big house go to ruin after he died."

Squirrel frowned at me, her eyebrows narrowing. I could tell she was getting frustrated with me. "So where are you going with all this? We heard it all before."

"You're right," I said. "But there's something else I noticed."

Squirrel rolled her eyes. "What?"

"Well, take a look at the Indian guide."

"What about him?"

"He's not standing there proudly beside Mackey and his daughter like I'd expect. He's not out of the picture, either, just a step or two back. Far enough to be a little out of focus. He's looking toward them, but it's hard to see his expression."

"It's just an old photo—probably from one of those old cameras. I don't know why you think it's such a big deal."

"I'm just curious, that's all. I wonder if the *Herald's* still got the original photo."

Squirrel looked at me like I was crazy. "I haven't got any more time for this," she said, refolding the paper and pushing it to one side. "I'm going to start dinner."

I had more to say, but I'd used up Squirrel's patience. Another idea had occurred to me, but it was pretty farfetched.

22

I gave some thought to calling Emma about the photo but decided to wait until I did a little poking around on the internet myself. I'm not a fan of technology, but like other older folks nowadays, I'd been dragged into the twenty-first century—though not without some kicking and screaming.

Before I retired from teaching, a new principal made all the teachers abandon their traditional gradebooks in favor of a software program called GradeQuick. I wasn't a willing convert, but I admit it had its plusses. I had always used a point system, carefully logging points earned on assignments into my gradebook. At the end of the marking period, I added up each student's points and arrived at a grade based on the percentage they'd earned of the total points possible.

Halfway through the marking period, I added up the students' points and issued progress reports. That was extra work, but it gave failing students a heads-up and a chance to bring up their grades before the marking period ended.

The software program changed all that. Once I entered the points in GradeQuick, it kept track of the total and indicated the students' percentages as new points were added. Suddenly there were no more arguments about grades. What was on the screen was the same as what I'd written in my gradebook, but seeing it on the screen made it real for the students in a way they could relate to.

Despite my reluctance to change my ways, that program saved me a lot of time and effort and settled a lot of arguments. I may not be a fan of change, but sometimes the reward for learning a new trick can make an old dog happy.

When Squirrel went out to the barn to tend to Flossie the

next morning, I headed upstairs to see just how farfetched my notion was. I didn't expect to capture lightning in a bottle exactly, but I hoped to at least shed some light on our mystery.

I booted up the computer and did a Google search for Noah Mackey. There were dozens of entries for the Landing's most famous citizen. I read a lengthy biography that told how Mackey was part of a group of Canadians that came to California during the Gold Rush. After a few years, he gave up on mining, cashed in on his early training in the north woods, and struck it rich as a lumberman.

The biography chronicled his business dealings and his contributions to civic improvements, notably the Mackey building with its upstairs theater, built in 1890 at a cost of over $100,000. The article made Mackey out to be the Landing's great benefactor, using his fortune on local undertakings, not for profit, but out of civic pride. I wondered what Earlene would have to say about that. Like she said, a lot depends on who's writing the history.

The article went on and on about his seemingly endless accomplishments, but I finally found what I was looking for near the end. I sat there for a moment, staring at the screen. My crazy idea wasn't so farfetched after all. Maybe it wasn't lightning in a bottle, but what I found confirmed my suspicions. I was onto something—finally. I printed out what I'd found. I couldn't wait to show it to Squirrel.

I heard a car and looked out to see Teddy's Scout pulling into the driveway. The truck rolled past the house and stopped at the barn. I watched as Dolly got out first, waiting for Teddy to come around and join her. The two headed out to the pasture, holding hands. The fair wasn't till the middle of August, and Dolly wouldn't be leaving for college until after that. They still had time together, but I knew they had more on their minds than parading their animals before the judges. I remembered the look on Teddy's face when he told me about his fear of losing Dolly to someone else. Sometimes, I thought, being old wasn't so bad.

I grabbed my printout and went downstairs. l was like the little kid who picked a flower in the woods and rushed home to show it to his mom, hoping she'd like it. I was hoping Squirrel wouldn't tell me I was all wet.

When I went around the back of the barn to the cow shed, Squirrel had let Flossie out into the pasture. She was leaning against the fence, talking with the two "lovebirds." The weekend was coming up and Squirrel was going over what needed to be done when the other kids arrived.

"Don't worry, Mrs. Barnes," I heard Dolly say. "Everything will be fine. Teddy and I will be here to help out."

"Hey, guys," I said when I caught up to them. "How are you doing?"

"We're fine," Teddy said. "We just wanted to go for a ride. Thought we'd stop and check on the stock. You know, make sure they've got water, toss out some feed, take a look around."

Squirrel and I looked after things when the kids weren't around, but it was typical of Teddy and Dolly to pitch in whenever they could. I hoped they'd stay on as adult volunteers when they were too old for 4-H. We talked a little more before the two went out to check on their animals.

"I think they just wanted an excuse to spend more time together," Squirrel said. "Charlie's fine and so is Dolly's lamb."

"You're probably right. Big changes ahead for sure, but they still have some time before school starts."

Squirrel looked at me, saw the paper in my hand. "So

what've you got there, Sherlock?"

"Remember that picture of Mackey in Emma's article?"

Squirrel gave me a doubtful look. "The one you thought was such a big deal? Of course."

"Well, it gave me an idea, so I looked Noah Mackey up on the internet. I had to wade through a lot of articles, but I finally found what I was looking for." I handed her the printout I'd been holding. "Here—take a look."

Squirrel held the page out in front of her and tilted it toward the light. I'd been in a hurry to show her what I'd found. I didn't think to bring her reading glasses.

She squinted at the page. "This is just a bio, stuff we already know."

"Keep reading," I said.

I was about to bust a gusset, waiting to see her reaction when she got to the end. When I finally saw her eyes light up, I knew she'd seen it, too.

"His daughter's name was Olive—how interesting!" Squirrel had jumped to the same conclusion as I had. She handed the page back to me. "I'm guessing you think she's our Olive, the one whose name is on the box."

"Don't you think so?"

She thought about it for a moment. "Could be just a coincidence," she said, letting a little air out of my sails. "It was probably a popular name back then."

"Maybe so, but Buck's Landing was pretty small in those days. Couldn't be that many girls named Olive."

"Probably not, but still…"

I could see the doubts creeping in. "I thought about it, too, but Mackey was rich. If someone gave his daughter a love token, it wouldn't be just some Cracker Jack toy. A fancy pendant in a silver box with her name on it would be just the right kind of thing."

Squirrel looked away, thinking it over. After a moment, she turned back, glanced at the printout in my hand, and looked up at me. "So what do we do now?"

"I'm still curious about the picture. I wonder what else Emma could find in the *Herald's* archives. I think we should give her a call."

"We should, huh? You mean I should call her. What do you want me to tell her?"

"Just tell her about the name. That will probably get her going. You know how she is. Ask her if she can find the original photo that accompanied the article. I want to take another look at it."

"Let's get dinner first," Squirrel said. She put her arm in mine as we walked back to the house. Teddy and Dolly were still out in the field somewhere. I wondered what the future had in store for them.

We talked some more over dinner. Squirrel's enthusiasm about my discovery lost a little of its edge the longer she thought about it. She seemed more interested in Teddy's and Dolly's predicament. I understood why Teddy was worried, but teen romance wasn't my biggest concern at the moment. It seemed like "girl talk"—just the kind of thing she and Emma would enjoy. I suggested she see what her sister had to say about it.

Squirrel gave me a knowing look. "You just want me to ask her about that picture."

She was right, of course. I didn't say anything more about it. I knew she'd get around to calling Emma, but she'd do it in her own time.

When dinner was over and the dishes were done, I went outside to put the chickens to bed. The older ones didn't need any help. When it was getting dark, they just strolled into the coop by themselves. They went to the door one at a time. Sometimes they pecked the ground a little, or stopped to flap their wings, but then they toddled up the ramp and hopped inside to roost. All I had to do was shut the door.

The Araucanas were a different story. The new girls hadn't quite got the hang of it. When I said, "Coop up, coop up," and tossed some mealworms inside, that would usually get them moving in the right direction. Once or twice, they'd actually gone in by themselves, probably anticipating that little treat. We were making progress.

I kept thinking about what I'd discovered—or what I thought I had. Was the Olive whose name was engraved on that silver box really Mackey's daughter? Or was that just some odd coincidence? Squirrel had her doubts, but I hoped it might be true. All those detectives in the movies say they don't believe in coincidences, but they happen all the time. Still, what would Mackey's daughter be doing on the south jetty beach at night? If she wasn't there, how did the box end up there where I could find it? It was baffling, to say the least. I shut the door on the Araucanas and headed back to the house.

Squirrel looked up as I came into the kitchen. She was sitting at the table, a steaming cup of coffee in front of her. She'd put some cookies out on a plate and was leafing through a copy of the *Farm Journal*.

"Coffee's still hot. Get a cup." She went back to her magazine, flipping a page. "The cookies are store-bought, but they're pretty good."

I was dying to ask what Emma'd had to say, but I poured myself a cup instead. I sat at the table, picked out a cookie, dipped it in my cup, and took a bite.

"The girls go to bed okay?" she asked.

"They're getting the hang of it," I said. "Probably go in on their own soon."

Squirrel was playing with me. She knew what I wanted to hear. She gave me a sideways look, an impish smile on her face. "Well?"

"Well what?" I couldn't wait any longer. "Did you call Emma? What did she say?"

"Don't go all crankypants on me, Billy. Of course I called her."

"Well what did she say?"

Squirrel toyed with the spoon in her coffee cup, then looked at me and smiled. "Actually, she seemed as excited as you are. She thought we were stuck, too, but her Nancy Drew radar's up and running again."

"What did she say about the picture?"

"She said she'd look into it, see what she could find. The pictures she used for her piece in the *Herald* were part of the articles when they were first published. She doesn't know if they still have the originals."

"She say anything else? I asked.

"Not much, but she seemed hopeful. 'They never throw anything away here' was the last thing she said."

A couple of days went by with no word from Emma. After taking time away for the special edition, she was probably back to work, digitizing the paper's archives. She was either too busy catching up with that, or else she couldn't find what we were hoping for. At any rate, the weekend was coming up, and there would be a lot to do when the junior members and their parents arrived to check on their projects.

We had 4-H papers spread out on the kitchen table Thursday evening when the phone rang. Squirrel was going over the junior members' record books, and we were planning what needed to be done over the weekend. Squirrel reached for the phone.

"Hello?" she said. She was still looking at the mess on the table, answering automatically. Her tone changed when she said, "Oh, hi Emma."

She turned to me and mouthed "It's Emma," as if I hadn't heard. She listened for a bit without saying anything. Finally, she said, "Sure… I think that would be fine." She listened a little longer. "Okay, then. Thanks for doing this."

That had to be the shortest conversation those two had ever had.

"What was that all about?" I asked.

"Emma sounds excited. She says she found something in the *Herald's* archives. She didn't explain. She and Frank are going away for the weekend, and she's got stuff to do at home, but she said if we come to her office in the morning, she'll show us what she found."

"She say anything else?" I asked.

"That's all she said. Frank was in the background, saying something. The two of them are always so busy. I think Emma's looking forward to their weekend getaway."

"I imagine she is," I said.

I admit I was a little jealous. Frank and Emma would cruise up the coast in the Land Rover to some quaint B&B perched on a bluff overlooking the ocean while Squirrel and I would be shoveling out the cow shed. But I didn't say anything.

"We should go to town in the morning," I said, "in case Emma plans on knocking off early."

"That's what she suggested—around ten o'clock. I told her that would be fine."

"I wonder what she has to show us."

Squirrel looked at the papers spread out on the table. "Whatever it is, we'll find out tomorrow."

23

We got up early, took care of the morning chores, and had a quick breakfast before we piled in the car and headed to town to meet up with Emma. Squirrel had taken forever getting ready, fussing over what to wear. She said she wanted to look nice when we showed up at Emma's. I wasn't exactly planning to walk in with cow flop on my shoes, but I wanted to get there before Emma left for the weekend. Squirrel assured me we had plenty of time as she made me change shirts a second time.

It was a cool morning, the overcast not yet burned off. Traffic slowed when we hit the main highway. The morning rush was on. It hadn't always been this way, but in the years since I'd retired, traffic had picked up considerably. It's not as bad as it is in bigger cities, I'm told, but it was another of those changes I like to complain about. We joined the steady stop-and-go as folks headed to work, and trucks bound for the mills on the other side of the bay inched along.

All the parking spaces were taken in front of the *Herald* building. We circled the block, hoping to find something further up the street. We found a spot on the same side of the street as the newspaper office, in front of the run-down mansion where the reclusive "cat lady" supposedly lived. The formal garden that once greeted visitors was sadly overgrown. The dead fronds hanging down against the trunks of the giant palms flanking the entrance rustled in the morning breeze. They hadn't been trimmed in ages. The whole place had a spooky look.

While we were still in the car, Squirrel took her cell phone out of her purse and called Emma to tell her we'd arrived, something that wouldn't have occurred to me. It made sense, though. I was slow to change, but working on it. In the old days, you had to find a phone booth to call someone when you were away from the house. Good luck with that nowadays.

The sour smell of the pulp mill washed over us as we got out of the car. We walked to the other end of the block, crossing the alley that ran between the old carriage house and the rear of the *Herald* building. When we got inside, Emma met us at the entrance to the elevator. As usual, she didn't waste any time on pleasantries.

"Come this way," she said. "I want to show you what I found."

She led us to a door at the end of the hall marked "Staff Only." She held the door open and we entered a small hallway. A door to the right had a lighted exit sign above it. To the left, a flight of stairs led down to a lower level. Emma flipped a switch, and we followed her down the stairs.

"Welcome to the 'tombs,'" she said, flipping on another switch. "It's what we call this place." She looked up at me. "Like I told Sorrel, they never throw anything away. It all ends up here."

It was a good-sized room with a big table in the center under a bright fluorescent panel. The beige-painted cinder-block walls were lined with file cabinets. Most of them were metal, the tan or gray kind you see everywhere, but some were the old-fashioned oak cabinets like they had in the library where Mom worked when I was a kid. Papers were stacked on top, and framed articles like the ones we'd seen in Emma's office hung above them. Without any windows, the room seemed airless and dank.

"Don't mind the musty smell," Emma said. "It bothered me at first, but I've spent a lot of time down here. I've gotten used to it. It's just old paper—smells a lot better than the pulp mill for sure."

Emma looked at us and smiled. "That's about it for the tour. Let me show you what I found."

She edged between the long side of the table and the metal file cabinets, heading toward the back of the room. It was darker in the back, away from the overhead light. She went to one of the oak cabinets, peered at the label, and moved to another beside it. Finding the one she wanted, Emma pulled out the drawer and rummaged inside. After flipping through some files, she pulled out a thick folder and brought it back to the table.

"Used to be a reporter on the *Herald* called Harold McBeth," Emma said, putting the folder on the table. "Everybody called him 'Hap.' He wrote a column for the paper called "Happy Landings," a play on his nickname and the name of the town. He hung out in the bars on Two Street, reported on local politics, dished up gossip on socialites and bigwigs like Noah Mackey. He was always around wherever Mackey showed up, followed him around like a puppy dog. He took pictures of him with a shovel, breaking ground for a new project or cutting the ribbon when a new building opened up."

"I remember seeing that column in the paper," I said, "but I didn't pay much attention to it back then. I was more interested in reading the funnies."

"He must have been quite a character," Squirrel said.

"Yeah," Emma continued. "Apparently Mackey took a liking to him, got used to having him around. Anyway, the two of them became friends it seems. Riding Mackey's coattails gave Hap plenty of fodder for his column, and Mackey probably liked all the free press he got.

"When Noah Mackey died in 1950, Hap continued his column until he died in a helicopter crash while covering the '64 flood. All his columns, with his notes and photos, were left at the *Herald*. When the paper moved from the office downtown to the new building, everything ended up here in the tombs."

Emma opened the folder on the table, leafing through some of the sheets inside.

I couldn't wait any longer. "Did you find what we're looking for?"

Emma threw us an apologetic look. "Sorry," she said. "I tend to get carried away."

Like when she's on the phone with Squirrel, I thought. "So, what did you find?"

"Well, Hap's whole career's in that file cabinet. I had to dig through a lot, but I finally found his notes for the article I used in the special edition. There are a lot of photos in there, too, but I managed to find the one we're looking for."

Emma pulled out a couple of photos, picked through them, and laid one out on the table. It was the photo we'd seen before, with Mackey and his daughter on the riverbank. Squirrel and I pulled out chairs and sat down. We got out our reading glasses to get a better look. Squirrel slid the picture closer, placing it between us.

The picture was a lot clearer than the tiny photo we'd seen in the newspaper. It was undoubtedly taken with one of those large-format cameras they used in the old days, not like the little pictures folks took with the 127 film in their Kodak Brownies.

Mackey had a big smile on his face, fish in one hand and his other clamped on his daughter's shoulder. She wasn't smiling. If anything, she looked gloomy, like she couldn't wait till it was over. In the background, the river guide stood in front of the boat, holding onto one of the oars stuck upright in the sand. He wasn't out of the picture, just far enough back to be a little out of focus. Still, it was clear to me that he looked about as unhappy as Olive.

Emma pointed to the picture. "Take a look at the back."

Squirrel turned the picture over. There was something written on the back in pencil. It was a little faded, but easy enough to read:

"On the river, 1938. Noah and Olive Mackey, with J. Whitehorse, river guide."

Squirrel and I looked at each other. Neither of us said anything for a moment. I looked at Emma. She just stood there, looking like the cat that got the cream.

"Well?" she asked.

"Well," Squirrel repeated, "I thought Billy was just grasping at straws when he wanted to get a look at the picture." She turned toward me. "But what you've found is really something."

"It explains a lot," I said. "Olive and Jacob must have met on one of those fishing trips Mackey was so fond of."

Emma had noticed the same thing I had. "Did you see the look on Jacob's face?" she asked.

"Yeah, he looks like he's ready to smack somebody with that oar."

"I think you're still reading a lot into it, Billy," Squirrel said. "Maybe he didn't want to be in the picture."

"Well, he's not really in the picture. He's just in the background, part of the scenery." I squinted at the photo again. "I think he doesn't like the way Mackey's holding the girl's shoulder. That grip looks almost painful."

"Now, I think you're getting carried away," Emma said, changing the subject. "Whatever else might be going on in that picture, it tells us who Jacob was and how he and Olive knew each other."

"Emma's right," Squirrel said. "I think we've found out what we wanted to know."

I thought about all that we'd learned. "It still doesn't

explain how that silver box ended up in the creek bed on the south jetty beach."

"We might never know the answer to that," Emma said. She put the photo back in the folder, straightened the papers inside, and closed it. It was clear she wanted to be done with us and finish her work so she could get a head start on the weekend. She returned the file to the oak cabinet and turned out the lights behind us as we headed up the stairs.

When we got to the top, Emma pointed to the exit door we'd seen earlier. "You can go out that way. It opens onto the alley. I've got to get back upstairs and finish some things before I leave."

Squirrel and I thanked Emma for finding the photo, still surprised at what we'd learned. She promised to let us know if she found anything else, though that seemed unlikely. She headed for the elevator, and we took the side door, leading to the alley.

We had some things to think about as we walked back to the car, but we didn't say much. The wind was up and blew down the alley toward us, kicking up some dust along with the smell of the pulp mill. I squinted and leaned into it, hoping to keep the dust out of my eyes. As we neared the walkway between the carriage house and the rundown mansion, I thought I saw someone slip between the buildings, headed inside. But when we passed by, the walkway was empty, and I didn't see anyone in the overgrown yard beyond the path. It was probably just my imagination. I wondered if my eyes were playing tricks on me.

Back in the car, we sat for a moment, thinking things over. As I waited for Squirrel to settle her purse on the floor and put on her seat belt, I looked out her window at the old house. It had worn that abandoned look as long as I could remember. As I sat there waiting for Squirrel, a hand parted the curtain in one of the front windows for just a second before it dropped back. Someone was watching us.

24

Squirrel was wrestling with her seat belt.

"Did you see that?" I asked. "See what?" she said, snapping the buckle in place.

"While you were fussing with your purse, I was looking at the cat lady's house. Somebody pulled back the curtain to look at us."

Squirrel looked out her window at the house. "Did you see who it was?"

"Just the hand parting the curtain. It was only there for a second or two. I almost thought I imagined it."

Squirrel looked at me, raising one eyebrow. "Maybe you did. I don't see anything over there."

"Well, they're gone now, but I know what I saw." I gave the mansion one last look as I started the car. The curtained windows stared back blankly at me. I checked the traffic and pulled out into the street.

We drove through town, not saying much. The morning traffic had thinned out, and I was thinking about what we'd learned from our visit with Emma. Squirrel must have been mulling it over, too.

"Well, I guess we know how Olive and Jacob met," she said. "I wonder how they managed to get any time alone together. Mackey always kept a close eye on her." She looked over at me. "Maybe she slipped away while her father was drinking with his buddies. Mackey liked to fish, made lots of trips up there. He probably hired Jacob more than once."

"I can see her sitting in that boat while Mackey's got his line in the water, the two of them making eyes at each other when the old man's not looking."

Squirrel thought about it for a moment. "Could be. Probably the only time Olive had a chance to be that close to a boy her age. And he was a good-looking guy, stocky but broad-shouldered—probably from all that rowing." There was a dreamy look in her eye when I glanced her way.

I let that perk for a while, putting the pieces together in my mind. We had some answers, but there were still a lot of gaps in the story. "So that picture was taken in 1938,' I said. "Those two were teenagers then. How do they end up on the south jetty in 1946?"

"Think about it, Billy. Olive tags along with her father on his trips to fish the Klamath. He does this for several seasons, and the two kids get to know each other, fall in love. Then the war happens. The first article Emma showed us said the man attacked on the beach was a soldier who'd recently returned from overseas."

I could see where she was going. "So Jacob joins the army, goes off to war. Maybe they keep in touch somehow. Absence makes the heart grow fonder and all that?"

"Why not?" Squirrel said. "After he comes home, they get together again. It could have happened just that way."

"So, what were they doing out there on the south jetty at night?"

"Jeez, Billy, what do you think? They were probably doing the same thing we were when we went out there."

I looked over at Squirrel, a little embarrassed. "I must be getting slow in my old age." I reached over and gave her knee a squeeze, remembering our night on the beach. "It sounds reasonable. If she was trying to get away from her old man for a while, the south jetty would be a good place for it."

I turned off the highway onto the Prairie Creek road. As we crossed the bridge over the slough, another thought occurred to me. "When we were in the alley on the way to the car, I thought I saw someone walk between the carriage house and the back of the mansion. There's a little walkway there between the buildings."

"Really? I didn't see anyone in the alley."

"I had my head down, squinting to keep the wind from blowing dust in my eyes. I was sure I saw someone, but when we got to the walkway, there was no one in sight."

"Well, I didn't see anyone. Maybe you're just seeing things, like the person you said you saw at the window."

"Maybe so," I said. Squirrel was probably right about that. She usually was. "But I know I saw someone pull back that curtain. I'm sure of that."

I could tell the wind was still with us when we got to the farm and turned into the drive. The windmill was spinning at a pretty fast clip, reminding me that it was time to climb up there and do my annual maintenance. I wasn't as fond of heights as I used to be, but I liked that windmill and did my best to keep it going. Maybe if I told Teddy what to do, he'd take care of it this year.

When we got out of the car, Squirrel headed into the house to rustle up something for lunch. I looked up again at the windmill and watched the white clouds scudding along overhead. If it wasn't the cat lady I saw, who was it? Dust in my eyes? Maybe that's all it was.

After lunch, we changed out of our town clothes and went outside. The sun was out and the wind had lost some of its enthusiasm. This was a good time of year, with fewer chores to be attended to. The hard work in the garden was done. The corn was up, and the purple blossoms on the pole beans had given way to the long purple pods I enjoyed seeing. The kids' pumpkins were coming along, too, sprouting green pumpkins everywhere. The way the vines were spreading, we might have to do some judicious pruning. We'd get larger pumpkins that way, making everybody happy.

We strolled over to the chicken yard and looked in on the chickens. When we'd let them out in the morning, we were rewarded with half a dozen eggs, two of them from the Araucanas. The new girls were pecking along the wire fence that separated them from the other chickens.

"I think it's time to let them in with the others," Squirrel said.

"That's fine with me. Let's see how they do."

I tossed out some scratch to give the other chickens something to think about while Squirrel opened the gate to let in the Araucanas. They kept pecking the ground along the fence even after the gate was open. Squirrel gave them a little nudge, heading them toward the opening in the fence. I tossed a little scratch their way, and they toddled into the main yard after the treat.

Nobody paid much attention to the newcomers until the scratch was gone. Penny, our banty hen, went over to take a look, pecking the ground beside them for leftovers. The other hens went about their business, apparently not interested in making new friends.

Our rooster'd had one red eye aimed at us the whole time. I'd been watching to see what he would do. Bobby Cantwell hadn't been his first victim. He'd come after me a time or two, and I'd learned not to turn my back on him. But I was only worried about the Araucanas at the moment.

The old boy strutted around a bit and flapped his wings, his wattles bouncing as he bobbed up and down. He danced over to the new girls, who were doing their best to ignore him. When he got closer, the Araucanas moved away. Penny rushed up and stood between them and the rooster. She squawked loudly and flapped her wings. I'd heard that sound before, a kind of distress call chickens make sometimes. The rooster cocked his head, training that beady eye on the little banty at his feet. They stared at each other for a moment or two. Finally, the big guy settled his wings and stalked off, pecking casually here and there in the yard.

"Looks like our girls have a new friend," Squirrel said.

"Yeah—that little banty hen sure put him in his place. It reminds me of that old saw that says it's not the size of the dog in the fight; it's the size of the fight in the dog. I guess it goes for chickens, too."

We decided to let things be in the chicken yard for a few hours. When it was time to put the chickens to bed, we'd put the Araucanas in their coop for the night and let them out in the yard with the others in the morning.

Somehow, all that drama in the chicken yard made me think about what we'd learned this morning. If our suspicions were correct, Olive and Jacob had picked a tough row to hoe. They'd needed someone like Penny to stand up for them and put that old rooster Noah Mackey in his place.

We left the chickens to fend for themselves and headed over to the barn. The fair was only a few weeks away, and there was a lot to do to get the animals ready. Tomorrow Squirrel and Dolly planned to show the older kids how to" block" their sheep to get them ready for the show ring, shearing them to emphasize their shape and structure. I helped her set up the fitting table in her classroom in the barn. It was a folding stand with a headpiece at one end. Once the sheep was on the stand with its head locked in place, grooming it was much easier. It was the same stand they used at the fair when they washed their animals before they went into the show ring.

I looked at the collection of old farm tools we'd hung on

the barn wall, spotting the hand shears Squirrel'd used when she was a girl. They were wicked-looking things—two long blades joined at the bottom. You squeezed them together like scissors to cut the wool. I'd tried them once, but couldn't make them work for me. Squirrel'd had lots of practice, and she'd made it look easy.

Those hand shears were another relic from the past. Nowadays we used an electric clipper, another change for the better. I took the shears down from the wall for a closer look.

"Remember these?" I said, squeezing the blades together a couple of times.

"Yeah, those things could raise blisters in a hurry," she said. "I always had to wear gloves." Squirrel looked at me and smiled. "Sure developed a heck of a grip, though."

Teddy would bring Dolly out with him in the morning. He was still working with Charlie, getting him to lead well and place his feet correctly. He'd promised to stop by Olsen's on the way and pick up a few bales of alfalfa and some sorghum. It was time to add some muscle and fat cover before Charlie went to auction. I'd lend a hand if needed, but I was pretty sure Teddy knew what he should do. Maybe I could even rope him into working on the windmill.

It was going to be a busy day. The parents would likely show up with food, and we'd have a nice lunch in the afternoon. I planned on taking it easy, hanging out with the junior members while they weeded the garden and took care of the chickens.

When we had everything ready, I went to the house for a pail of warm water while Squirrel let Flossie into the cow shed. The wind had died down, as it often did in the evening. When I got back, Squirrel washed her up, pulled the three-legged stool over, and set the milk pail in place. Flossie raised her head, a wisp of hay hanging from her mouth. She gave me a dismissive look and continued chomping away.

I watched the two of them as Squirrel rested her forehead against Flossie's flank and squirted the milk into the pail. I leaned against the wall, letting my thoughts wander through the day's events. Emma'd helped us fill in some of the gaps in the story of Olive and Jacob, and Squirrel had convinced me that she knew what they were doing on the beach that night. But why did Jacob end up beaten and left for dead? And if the silver box with the pendant was theirs, how did it end up in the creek bed?

25

We spent the next few weeks getting ready for the fair. It was a big deal for us. Most folks who stroll through the exhibits plucking at their cotton candy don't realize all the work that's involved.

Squirrel and Dolly had checked the junior members' accounts and updated everything. Entry forms had been submitted to the fair office, and Dolly's father had "volunteered" one of his friends who owned a truck to haul the larger animals to the fairgrounds.

Olson's feed store always sets up shop at the fair, selling everything from chicken feed to rabbit pellets. Teddy would haul some hay and feed in his Scout, but if we needed anything else, we could count on Olson's.

Vendors and exhibitors who came from out of town parked their vehicles in the back lot at the fairgrounds. They usually slept out there in their RVs or the trailers they towed behind their pickup trucks. Teddy planned to sleep in the Scout to keep an eye on the animals and watch over our stuff.

Dolly had wanted to camp out with Teddy, but her mother wouldn't hear of it. "It's not safe," she told them. There'd be a lot of folks camping on the back lot, many of them strangers, but I figured Dolly's safety wasn't Lorna Aguirre's first concern. She was more worried about what those two kids might be getting up to in the back of Teddy's truck.

Maybe she was right. Squirrel and I'd been young once, too. We knew how those kids felt about each other, but we'd never been parents. Still, Lorna couldn't keep Dolly tied to her apron strings forever.

Besides helping the kids ready their projects and deal

with the livestock, we had to make sure the 4-H booth would be ready, with photos of the members' projects and brochures to hand out.

Most of the booths in the commercial building had something to give to visitors. The Forest Service gave out pencils imprinted with Smokey Bear and the "Only You Can Prevent Wildfires" slogan. When we were kids, Smokey told us, "Remember… Only You Can Prevent Forest Fires." Now it was "wildfires." It always seemed to me that "wildfires" were mostly caused by lightning, but who am I to argue? Smokey is a favorite with everybody.

Businesses selling everything from cookware to garden supplies gave out balloons, hot pads, wooden rulers, all imprinted with the name of the company. The idea was to attract attention and encourage visitors to stop and chat with the vendors.

The 4-H wasn't to be outdone. This year, we had keychains with the 4-H clover emblem and some pinback buttons to give out, along with the brochures explaining all the 4-H programs and membership information.

Squirrel and I'd also had some flyers printed up to tell folks about the fall events on our farm—our annual pumpkin patch activities, the hayrides on weekends, apples and cider for sale—that sort of thing. It was a little shameless self-promotion that brought in some needed revenue.

Things were coming together, and we had a little time to relax. This morning, after breakfast, Squirrel was making butter. I brought the electric churn in from the cupboard in the laundry room and set it on the counter by the sink. I asked if she needed my help.

"When I was a girl, Emma and I took turns cranking the Dazey churn. She was too little, so I did most of the work, but I let her take a turn when my arm got tired."

"The churn that's out in the barn with the old farm tools," I said. It was a big glass jar with wooden paddles that spun around inside when you turned the crank on top. "Must have been kinda fun, though, watching the cream turn into butter."

"Yeah, it was—kind of like magic. But it took a long time. The magic wore off pretty fast." Squirrel unscrewed the motor from the top of the churn, laying it on the counter. She poured in the cream and set the cream pitcher in the sink. She looked at me and smiled. "This one might not be so much fun, but it's faster and a lot easier on the arm."

It was another of those changes that made sense, no matter how stuck I was in the old ways. Squirrel didn't need a helper to turn the crank, so I decided to take a walk through the orchard. It was a nice morning—sunny, but still a little cool—so I grabbed a hat and headed out the back door.

The Red June apples were gone now, turned into pies and cobblers we'd enjoyed and given away to friends and relatives. The other varieties were coming along. We seemed to have won the battle with the codling moths—for now, at least.

We'd been too busy lately to spend more time trying to unravel the story of Olive and Jacob. I didn't think Squirrel was giving it any thought at all. She seemed happy enough with what we'd discovered, but I wished we knew the whole story. I was like a dog with a bone, carrying it around with me all the time, chewing on it every once in a while.

We'd learned a lot when we visited Emma at the *Herald*. We knew how Olive and Jacob met, and it didn't take long for Squirrel to figure out what they were doing on the south jetty at night. She seemed content with what we'd learned, but that wasn't the end of the story.

Then there was that creepy business at the cat lady's

house. I don't know why it spooked me up so much. I'd heard stories about that house since I was a kid, but I'd never really paid much attention. When we'd driven past there one day, my dad told me those stories were just gossip, people making up tales to match their imaginations. Everyone said an old lady lived there. She was rich once, but fell on hard times, dismissed her servants, and settled in with her cats, letting the place go to ruin. No one had set eyes on her in years.

Since Squirrel hadn't seen what I had with her own eyes, she thought I was making the whole thing up. I was probably reading too much into it, but I know I saw someone at that window. I had jumped to the conclusion that we were being watched, but by now I'd decided that was just plain silly. If someone were looking out the window, it was probably just the cat lady looking to see who was parking in front of her house.

When I got back to the kitchen, Squirrel was just finishing up. She'd poured out the buttermilk left in the jar and transferred the butter to a large bowl, added salt, and was packing it into waxed cartons to store in the freezer. Salted butter might be bad for you, but it tasted better and lasted longer.

"I'm almost done," she said. "Could you give me a hand with the churn?"

When I dipped my finger in the bowl to sample the butter, Squirrel slapped my wrist. "Stay out of there," she said.

"Just checking," I said, licking my finger. I picked up the empty jar she'd set in the sink and carried it out to the laundry room, setting it in the laundry tray. I squirted in some dish soap and filled the big jar with warm water. Washing out the jar and cleaning the paddles was awkward and messy, but I didn't mind. That butter I'd licked from my finger had tasted really good.

With our booth set up and manned by junior members and parent volunteers, Squirrel and I found some time to take in the sights at the fair. Teddy and Dolly were taking care of things in the livestock barn and the poultry house. The kids were happily chatting with visitors about their animals, and everything seemed to be under control. The livestock judging wouldn't take place for a few days, and it was nice to be on our own for a couple of hours.

We bought a couple of corn dogs and a basket of fries and walked over to the stage where local performers entertained in the afternoon. We sat at one of the picnic tables set up on the lawn. Two guys were giving their rendition of Johnny Cash's "Tennessee Flat Top Box," and a crowd had gathered to watch. They were enjoying themselves—"folks from nine to ninety," like the song says, tapping their toes and nodding their heads.

The young man doing the singing might dream of making the Hit Parade like the dark-haired boy in the song, but I thought his chances were slim. His singing was passable, but he was no Johnny Cash. He just strummed the rhythm guitar as he sang, but the old guy with the steel-stringed acoustic guitar was something else. When he came in between the choruses, he stole the show.

After lunch, we headed over to look at the displays in the exhibit building. Squirrel always wanted to see the quilts and handcrafts. The quilts weren't really my thing, but the woodworking exhibits and the artifacts on display by the historical society were always interesting.

The carnival had set up behind the exhibit building, between it and the grandstand. The big attractions would take place on the weekend, when folks came from all around for the mule races and the rodeo events. It was Tuesday, and things were pretty slow. It would be different when the grandstand was filled, and the carnival's neon lights were on, casting their magic on the midway.

The Ferris wheel turning overhead reminded me of when Squirrel and I rode the big wheel as teenagers. We were just getting to know each other then. With Squirrel beside me and the rest of the world spread out below us, it was magical, even in the daytime without the neon lights. *Those were the days, my friend…* I took Squirrel's hand in mine as we walked along, headed toward the commercial building.

Shiny new tractors were displayed on the lawn outside the building, along with riding mowers, log splitters, and chainsaws. A sales rep was talking with two middle-aged men, one of them in strap overalls. The other guy looked like a logger, with a chambray work shirt and Ben Davis jeans held up by wide suspenders. He was a big guy, with a wad of tobacco tucked in his cheek. The logger was squinting at a brochure. The salesman grinned, patting the handle on a Stihl chainsaw. "Can't go wrong with one of these," he said.

Inside, the main room was taken up with vendors showing off their products, everything from locally produced jams and jellies to satellite dishes. A fellow in the center aisle with a headset and a microphone was hawking pots and pans to a few folks who'd settled in the folding chairs in front of his booth. Elsewhere, booths displaying water purifiers, cell phones, kitchen cabinets, and garden fountains vied for visitors' attention. Squirrel and I looked at things here and there, finally succumbing to the fudge and divinity from the Fudge Factory before we left the main room.

Service providers and community groups were located in another room, away from the hustle and noise of the bigger vendors. Plumbers, electricians, garden and house cleaning services were mixed in with representatives from the Boy Scouts, the Highway Patrol, and the Fish and Game Department. Our 4-H booth shared the room with those folks, along with community action groups like Save the Bay and the Indian cultural center.

Things were under control at the 4-H booth when we checked in. Like everyone else, we'd get busier with the weekend crowds. Alan Scott's mom, one of the parent volunteers, said some folks had dropped by, and they'd handed out a few brochures. Alan, a nine year-old junior member, looked cute in his green hat and tie, but I could tell he was getting fidgety. He brightened up considerably when Squirrel offered him a piece of our fudge.

I'd been hoping to talk to Earlene. Squirrel didn't want to bother her, but I was eager to tell Earlene what we'd learned since we last spoke with her. Doris, the woman we'd seen when we were in Earlene's office, was sitting in the cultural center booth, but there was no sign of Earlene. I figured she was busy at the center downtown. I knew she'd show up sooner or later. She'd want to let folks know about the social services the center offered and gather support for her causes.

I remembered the look on Earlene's face when she closed the silver box and handed it back to us. She'd seen that name on the top, and it meant something to her. I was convinced she was holding back something. I wondered what she knew and wasn't telling us.

We got busier as the week moved along, but every time we checked on our booth in the commercial building, I kept an eye out for Earlene. I really wanted to talk to her, but she was never there when we were. She certainly knew we'd be at the fair. I began to think maybe she was trying to avoid us, but that seemed silly, too. Her work at the center was too important to keep her away.

Doris was there every day, sometimes with another staff member, but there was no sign of Earlene. Finally I went over to poke my nose in and have a chat with Doris. I reminded her that we'd met briefly when Squirrel and I were in Earlene's office. I said I was surprised that Earlene wasn't there. We'd been friends forever, and we were hoping to visit with her during the fair.

Doris just said something had come up that needed Earlene's attention. She didn't explain any further, and I didn't push it. Whatever was keeping Earlene away must be pretty important, but it was none of my business. Still, it made me curious.

26

The Junior Livestock auction was held on Saturday, and the kids had been busy scurrying around the barns feeding, bathing, and grooming their animals to prepare for the big event. The auction was always popular, and the crowd had gathered early, filling the bleachers that surrounded the show ring with spectators and prospective buyers.

The auction started at nine in the morning, with Aubrey Winter, the auctioneer, warming up the audience with his folksy charm. He was a gray-haired windbag, but everybody loved him. He wore his usual western shirt with pearl buttons and a string tie with a silver-mounted turquoise clasp. A matching belt buckle held up the boot-cut jeans. Snakeskin shit kickers completed his outfit. He'd been doing this for years, keeping up a steady patter as he tried to get folks to pay up and reward the kids for their hard work. Buyers at the fair expected to pay more than grocery store prices in order to support the livestock program, and Aubrey did his best to get kids better than break-even money—profits that could go toward college savings or be spent on next year's animal.

Aubrey seemed to be in fine form as we passed by the show ring on our way to see how our kids were doing out in the barns. The top eight animals—the grand champion and reserve champion hog, lamb, steer, and goat—would be auctioned off in the afternoon, attracting the biggest crowd. Squirrel and I would be there to see that, too.

Teddy and Dolly hadn't fared that well in the judging, but they'd done all right. They'd each gotten a blue ribbon to show their animals exceeded minimum standards, but no rosettes to denote Grand or Reserve Champion winners.

Dolly seemed happy with how things turned out, but Teddy had hoped to do better. The top animals would fetch higher prices, and he'd been hoping to set aside some money for college.

"I think he'll make out all right," Squirrel said. "Mr. Winter knows how to get the best prices for the kids."

"Get a couple of guys trying to outbid each other like he does sometimes. That would help, for sure."

Dolly was busy grooming her sheep when we checked on her, but she assured us that everything was fine, and we headed out to the cow barn to see how Teddy was doing. We walked along the row of stalls, the line of swishing tails waving as we passed by. Teddy was sitting on a bale of hay, leaning against the side wall of Charlie's stall, a bottle of Gatorade in his hand. Charlie was munching contentedly on a sprig of alfalfa. The steer turned his head to look at us, but lost interest right away and turned back, more interested in the hay.

"Hey, Teddy. How are you doing?" I said.

He looked up at us, smiling. "I'm fine. It's all good. How are things over at the booth?"

"Everything's fine over there," Squirrel said. "It's early yet, but we've already had quite a few visitors this morning."

Teddy seemed in remarkably good spirits, which surprised me. He was always such a worrier. I think Squirrel saw it, too. She gave him a concerned look. "You worried about the auction?"

Teddy looked up at us then, a little smile beginning to show. "Not really. I hoped Charlie'd do better, but it's okay. Everything's going to be okay now."

Something was on his mind, and it wasn't the price of livestock. Squirrel glanced at me and turned back to study

Teddy. "You look like you're sitting on a secret. You know something we don't?"

The smile got wider. "Yeah—but it's not about the auction. Dolly and I've been talking, trying to work things out. Her going off to Davis had me tied in knots, like I told you earlier."

"I remember," I said. "You're not worried now?"

"She's not going!" Teddy said, grinning. "At least not right away. She's going to go to Buck's next year. She figures she can get her general ed. requirements out of the way in the first two years, and then transfer in as a junior."

"Not a bad plan," Squirrel said. "It'll save her some money, for sure."

"And we can still be together while we figure things out."

"Well," I said, "Congratulations. Things do have a way of working out sometimes. We'll keep our fingers crossed. Meanwhile, don't forget about the auction. Be sure Charlie gets to the show ring on time."

"Don't worry, we'll be there. Everything's going to be fine."

Squirrel and I headed back to the commercial building to check on the 4-H booth. We strolled across the fairgrounds, taking in the sights. We looked in on the historical society's little cabin set up with artifacts from pioneer life. Black iron skillets and a couple of sad irons, those heavy cast iron ones with the wooden handles, were laid out on a woodburning stove. A ladder-back rocking chair stood in one corner beside a painted iron bedstead with the quilt folded back to show the blue-and-white mattress ticking underneath. An older lady decked out in a prairie bonnet and gingham apron chatted with visitors, eager to answer questions.

Outside, we stopped to look at the display of hit-and-miss

engines farmers once used to power everything from water pumps to washing machines. They were colorful engines with big flywheels that maintained engine speed as the crankshaft turned between power strokes. Local collectors loved to demonstrate their restored engines, firing them up to please fairgoers. Most of the onlookers were men, and I could tell Squirrel wasn't too interested. When I pointed out a green Maytag washing machine engine puffing smoke, she said, "Imagine that noisy thing in your laundry room, belching out smoke like that."

"I think you stick the exhaust pipe out the window," I said. I could tell she wasn't a fan.

When we got back to the commercial building, Bobby Cantwell and his mom were holding down the fort at the 4-H booth. Betty Cantwell looked a little frazzled. They'd been there for a couple of hours, and Bobby was starting to get fidgety. The first thing he said was, "Where's Dolly?"

Knowing how he worshiped her, I could imagine his disappointment when she wasn't in the booth when they arrived. "She's out in the barn with her lamb." I said. "Why don't you and your mom go out and see the animals?"

Betty gave us a relieved look. "Thank you," she said.

"It's fine, Squirrel said. "We'll take over for a while. Go look around, maybe get Bobby some cotton candy." Bobby brightened up considerably when she said that.

"Thanks for helping out in the booth," I said.

Whenever I was in the building, I looked for Earlene, but she was never around. I kept expecting her to show up, but the fair was almost over, and I hadn't seen her once. When Doris saw me looking her way, she just shrugged her shoulders, telling me she didn't know anything new. That made me wonder even more.

From the way she'd acted earlier, I was pretty sure Earlene kept things to herself, but she and the others at the cultural center worked together every day. I figured Doris probably knew more than she was letting on.

Squirrel thought I was just being nosy. "It's none of our business," she said. "Earlene's got her own problems to deal with, just like everybody else. You can tell her what we learned at Emma's the next time we see her—after the fair's over."

Squirrel was right, of course. We had a lot of other things to do right now.

Teddy and Dolly did well at the auction. They were good-looking kids who handled their animals well in the show ring, obviously proud of their work. Aubrey Winter worked up the bidders, getting a good price for both of them. Charlie sold for a hefty $3.00 a pound, more than we expected, and well above the break-even point. Teddy and Dolly would both turn a profit at the fair this year.

Squirrel and I went with the kids to meet the buyers and sign the papers. When that was done and Teddy and Dolly received their checks, the buyers would arrange for the animals to be transported and harvested. Then they would be sent to a butcher shop for a custom cut and wrap before being sent frozen to the buyer. All those services were paid for by the customer, which added a lot to the price, but folks were willing to step up to show their support for the program.

Most of Sunday was spent winding down and starting to pack up. Teddy and Dolly said good-bye to their animals and loaded our things from the barn into the Scout. Dolly didn't seem too upset about giving up her sheep, but Teddy'd gotten attached to that steer. When he patted Charlie on the cheek for the last time, he turned away, wiping his nose on his sleeve. He didn't look back as he and Dolly walked away.

Dolly took her arm in his, and they headed toward the carnival. They spent the afternoon there, enjoying the rides and each other's company. Squirrel and I managed to take an hour off to watch the mule races while Carla Spencer and her dad served their shift in the booth.

At the end of the day, we finished packing and headed home, tired but happy, knowing things had gone well. We had signed up some new prospects for next year, and Teddy and Dolly would stick around as adult volunteers, at least for now. We still had chores to tend to, but I was hoping to find some time just to sit on the porch and watch the clouds go by.

27

We enjoyed having a break from the flurry of activities surrounding the fair. We still had our daily chores, but the slower pace was refreshing, and we spent the next few weeks puttering around the farm.

Teddy and Dolly stopped by once in a while, but we didn't see a lot of them. They were settling in at the local college and seemed to be getting along okay. Dolly was harder to read, but Teddy appeared to have jumped in with both feet, proudly wearing his new green sweatshirt with the Buck's State logo the last time we saw them. Registration had been hectic, he said, but they had managed to get two of their classes together. Dolly stood beside him, her arm linked in his, but she didn't say much. She just smiled as Teddy rattled on about school. I hoped things would work out for them.

The pumpkins in the garden had grown, turning orange, a reminder that fall was on its way. Apple-picking time would soon be upon us, and I spent some time getting ready. I went through our store of wooden apple boxes, left over from past days when we sold apples in them. Nowadays, they were impossible to come by, but we still used them when we picked the fruit, laying the boxes out on the old flatbed trailer Squirrel's father had made. Folks who bought our apples these days either brought their own cardboard boxes or took the apples home in paper bags.

I cleaned up the cider press and got down the three-legged ladders and canvas picking sacks, making sure we had everything we needed. The soda shop in town used to give us the glass jugs the Coke syrup came in when they were empty, but everything came in plastic now, so we had to buy our own—plastic, too, of course. Squirrel'd had some labels printed up with the Posey farm name, which was something we hadn't had before, and she'd ordered a large custom-made rubber stamp to put our name on the paper bags.

With a little free time, Squirrel and I talked about taking a day trip somewhere while the weather was still good. Flossie and the chickens pretty much tied us to the farm, but a day trip was a possibility.

"We need to take a day off, Billy," Squirrel suggested one morning during breakfast.

"Sounds good to me," I said. "Got anything in mind?"

Squirrel twirled the spoon in her coffee cup, set it on the napkin, and looked up at me. "I just want to go somewhere while the weather's still nice." She paused, thinking. "Maybe we could go to the beach."

"Not another trip to the south jetty."

"No—up north a ways, where we used to go—that beach with the tide pools. Remember?"

"I do." Hermit Beach was very small, hemmed in by rocky bluffs and accessible only by a steep trail, but the hike down had been worth it when we were younger. "You have to be part mountain goat to navigate that trail. You think we're still up to it?"

Squirrel smiled. "Only one way to find out."

I put the lunch Squirrel packed into the trunk of the car, along with a blanket to sit on. I pushed the metal detector aside to make room. My SE Pro had taken up residence there after the trip to the south jetty, but I was done hunting for treasure on the beach, at least for now.

We put on light jackets and headed north after the morning chores were done. The new freeway was faster, but we took the old road, puddling along the way we'd gone when we were kids. We weren't in a hurry, and it was a nice drive through areas we hadn't seen in ages.

North of the Landing, the old highway went up a hill, passing through a wide spot in the road with a gas station and a couple of stores. Beyond that, the airport that handled commercial flights in and out of Buck's Landing spread out to the west. There was a gun club out there, too, on the bluff overlooking the ocean. I'd been there once with my dad and his friend when they had gone to a "turkey shoot." I was little then and thought they were going to shoot turkeys. It turned out to be a skeet shooting competition. The winner got a turkey for Thanksgiving.

The other thing I remembered from that trip was the concrete bunkers on the edge of the bluff. My dad explained that they were left over from the war, built to hold weapons to ward off the Japanese if they reached the west coast. Military aircraft from the airport flew training missions back then, using a range set up on an isolated beach further north for target practice. Dad took me there once, too, and we'd spent some time poking around in the sand, digging up some big copper bullets and a couple larger shells.

I thought about all that as we drove along the narrow road, the ocean on our left, visible through the trees now and then. Squirrel and I'd been born during the war, but it was over by the time we were old enough to remember things. The war wasn't very far in the past for our parents, though. They never talked about it very much, probably eager to put it behind them.

I learned a few things as I got older. I knew there'd been some incidents along the west coast, and the Coast Guard had patrolled the beaches on horseback day and night to prevent sneak attacks on isolated stretches. There were big battles way up north in the Aleutians, but we'd been left alone for the most part. I knew about the balloon bombs the Japanese sent our way toward the end of the war when they were pretty desperate. Most of those never made it very far, but a couple of them managed to get through. One of them came down on Hupa land.

That thought made me think of what we'd learned about Olive and Jacob. When I tried to bring up the subject, Squirrel wasn't interested in talking about it.

"Let's just enjoy the day," she said. "We hardly ever get a chance just to take the day off and do something different."

Hermit Beach was pretty much as we remembered it, a narrow spit of sand between two tall bluffs. Sea stacks—big rocks, some with scrubby trees on top—rose out of the ocean offshore. The tide was out, revealing rocky pools between the sandy beach and the nearest of the offshore rocks.

The beach was unchanged, reminding me of Longfellow's "The Tide Rises, the Tide Falls," his poem about the immutability of nature, but "the little waves with their soft white hands" hadn't managed to erase all the footprints from the sands. The terrible trail down to the beach had been improved over the years, with steps cut into the hillside here and there, and even some railings installed on switchbacks with steep drop-offs. No more mountain goats. Even an old goat like me could make it down to the beach.

Ice plants, wild strawberries, and scrubby bushes lined the path as we picked our way down the new trail. It was a lovely day, one of those warm September days when you first notice it seems to get dark a little earlier, and the cooler breeze in the late afternoon sends you looking for the jacket you didn't need when you left the house. We spread out the blanket, and Squirrel unpacked our lunch, handing me an egg salad sandwich and a can of Coke.

We looked out at the sea as we ate, pointing out the gulls wheeling overhead and a lone pelican, which reminded Squirrel of her mom, who used to tell the girls, "A wonderful bird is the pelican. His beak can hold more than his belly can."

I'd heard that one, too. It was an old limerick. The rest of it said "He can hold in his beak, enough food for a week! But I'll be darned if I know how the hellican."

We laughed over that as we finished our lunch and headed down to the water's edge to explore the tide pools. On the sandy beach, the waves tumbled against the shore, a steady pleasant sound. Among the rocks, the waves splashed up, refilling the pools, then draining away before the next ones came. The tide was beginning to turn, and we kept a lookout for bigger waves that could drench us as we investigated the tide pools.

When the tide was out, there was a lot to see. Squirrel pointed out a hermit crab in a borrowed shell scuttling across the bottom of one of the pools. Orange and purple starfish clung to the rocks on the edges. Squirrel scolded me when I pried one off to look at the underside. "Put it back, Billy," she said.

"I just wanted to see underneath."

People used to take starfish and other things home from the beach to hang on their cabin walls. Maybe they still do, but I knew better. I studied the little grippers on the bottom, then carefully put the guy back where I found him.

Sea anemones blossomed in the shallow pools, their fringed edges waving as the pools drained and refilled. I remembered being fascinated by them when I was little. I poked one with my finger, watching it close up, responding to my touch. Tiny ones of a different type carpeted some of the smaller rocks. They squirted water at you when you pressed on them.

Squirrel gave me a look, so I quit messing with the anemones. I looked out to sea while she checked out another pool. I stood there, taking in the salty air and watching the waves, each one a little different from the last. I watched as the turning tide crept further up the shore, ready to shout a warning if a big wave came.

I thought about other times when we'd visited this beach, and the fun we'd had, wading in the foam at the edge of the waves, holding hands as the receding wave pulled at our feet, then laughing as we dashed back up the beach when the next one rolled in

I watched Squirrel as she explored the tide pool. Barefoot, her jeans rolled up to her knees, she still stirred my heart. We were growing old together, but she would always be the red-haired girl that left me speechless when she sat beside me on the school bus one morning.

I looked back at the pool with the anemones. I thought about how they closed up when you poked them. It made me think of how Earlene had closed up when she first saw Olive's name on that silver box. Before that, she'd told us a lot about the pendant and the Hupa word on the back, but when she put it back in the box and closed the lid, she'd seen the name and clammed up. I chuckled over that one—"clammed" up—and me on the beach! I still maintained Earlene was avoiding us, but Squirrel thought she was just busy with other things.

I didn't want to spoil our day at the beach, so I didn't say anything to Squirrel. She might have put the mystery to rest, but it was still nagging at me. Earlene hadn't told us all she knew, and I wanted to know what she was hiding.

We stayed at Hermit Beach long enough to watch the waves swallow up the tide pools before we packed up our things and headed to the car. The hike up the hill wasn't as easy as it'd been coming down, and we stopped a couple of times to catch our breath. Leaning against the railing on one of the switchback turns, we looked back at Hermit Beach and the sea beyond.

"It's really beautiful here," Squirrel said, putting her arm around me. "I'm really glad we came."

"Me, too," I said.

Back at the car, we emptied the sand out of our shoes, and tossed our things into the trunk. I got behind the wheel, and we headed home. We took the old road again, in no hurry for the day to end.

We couldn't help but notice the changes that had taken place. Land along the coast hadn't been all that desirable in the forties and fifties, and people with modest means had built small houses among the trees on the hills above the beach. Some of them even had ocean views.

Times had changed, and places along the coast had become hot properties. People with champagne tastes had pushed aside the folks with beer foam pocketbooks, and a lot of the old homes were gone now, replaced by fancier houses, even if they didn't have an ocean view.

An enterprising fellow with plenty of money had built an upscale restaurant on one of the bluffs overlooking the ocean. People who could afford it treated themselves to fine dinners at Marino's while they sipped cocktails and watched the sun sink into the sea.

Despite the changes, it was still a lovely drive along the old highway and Squirrel and I were having a good time. "Taking a day off was a great idea," I told her. "I'm glad you suggested it."

"Thanks. It was nice to get out of the house for a change."

"Hermit Beach was fun. We hadn't been there in years."

Squirrel's cell phone chimed as we neared the airport.

Cell service was non-existent at the isolated beach and spotty along the old highway, but apparently someone had sent her a text while we were out of range. Squirrel dug her phone out of her purse to see what it was.

Ít's from Emma," she said.

"What did she have to say?"

Squirrel had a puzzled look on her face.

"It just says, 'Call me.'"

28

Squirrel was staring at her phone, her eyebrows narrowed. "That's all it says?" I asked. "Just 'Call me'?"

Squirrel nibbled on her bottom lip. "Yeah."

Emma's cryptic text sounded ominous, but I tried to reassure Squirrel. "It's probably nothing serious. Maybe she just wanted to talk."

"I don't know, Billy. She usually says what's on her mind. I hope it's nothing terrible."

I thought about it for a few seconds. "Only one way to find out. Call her back."

I knew what Squirrel was going through. The more I thought about Emma's two-word text, the more I thought it likely something bad had happened. My heart thumped in my chest, and a trickle of sweat rolled down my back. What if there'd been an accident and Frank or one of their kids had been hurt?

I watched the road as Squirrel scrolled through the contacts in her phone and called her sister. "Put it on speaker," I said.

Emma answered on the second ring. "Where've you been?" she said. As usual, she was all business. When Squirrel's number showed up on her phone, she didn't bother with the formalities. "I've been trying to get ahold of you."

"We were at the beach, didn't get your message till we were back on the highway. Is everything okay? Are you all right?"

"I'm still at the *Herald*. I'm fine, but something's up at the old mansion next door."

Squirrel's shoulders lost their tension as she settled back

in her seat, relieved. "What do you mean? What's going on?"

"I was working in my office when all hell broke loose. I can't see anything from my room, but I heard a commotion in the hall and went out to see what was going on. People on the side of the building facing the alley were bunched up at the windows. Someone had seen the sheriff's car pull up next to the carriage house. The sheriff got out and went into the yard, headed toward the back of the big house.

"Skip Mallory, one of the reporters, went over to see what was going on. He disappeared into the gap between the buildings and came back a few minutes later with the sheriff. The two of them stood by the sheriff's car talking, and after a few minutes, the coroner's wagon pulled into the alley."

"So the cat lady must have died," Squirrel said, stating the obvious.

"Yeah. Skip's over there getting all the details. It's why I called. I thought you'd like to know."

"Well, of course," I said. "We always wondered what went on over there."

"I'll let you know what Skip has to say when he comes back. Meanwhile, everybody at the paper's digging into the archives to see what they can come up with about the cat lady and her house for the next edition. I'll call you later if they turn up anything."

Squirrel thanked Emma and ended the call. "Well, that was interesting," she said.

"Yeah. I was afraid something had happened, but I couldn't imagine what it might be."

"Well, something did happen, didn't it?"

"Yeah." I thought about it for a moment. "Everybody knows about the rundown mansion and the crazy lady with the cats. We all heard the story growing up, accepted it as fact. Filed it away in our minds and didn't think any more about it."

"She wasn't just the 'cat lady,' Billy. She was a real person."

"I know," I said. "I wonder what Emma's people will find to say about her."

I thought about Emma's call as we drove back to the farm. Squirrel was right, of course.

The mansion, with its overgrown gardens and rundown façade, was a relic from another time, a monument left over from an earlier age, but the woman who'd lived there all those years was a real person with her own story. I wondered what Emma's friend Skip and the others at the *Herald* would come up with.

Back at home, we put away our things from the trip and took care of the evening chores. I went outside after dinner to put the chickens up for the night while Squirrel cleared the table and started doing the dishes.

When I got back to the house, she had the dishes in the rack and was scrubbing out the sink with cleanser. I grabbed a tea towel and started drying the dishes. The phone rang as she was rinsing the sink.

"Why don't you get that while I finish up?" I said. "It might be Emma."

Squirrel dried her hands and got to the phone on the third ring.

"Hello," she said. She looked my way, nodded, and mouthed, "It's Emma."

I went to work on the dishes, listening with one ear, but there wasn't much to hear. Emma seemed to be doing all the talking. I wished she'd called on the cell phone, so we could put it on speaker. There was an extension in the bedroom, but I was busy with the dishes, and I knew Squirrel would tell me what Emma had to say anyway.

I looked over at Squirrel. She was nodding her head,

listening intently.

"Really?" she said. She listened a few moments longer, her eyes widening in surprise. "That's really interesting." She covered the mouthpiece with her hand and looked at me. "Wait till you hear what Emma found out," she said.

I finished drying the dishes and put them away while Squirrel and her sister talked a while longer. Squirrel didn't say much besides, "Wow" and "We had no idea." I was dying to know what Emma was saying. Finally, Squirrel said, "Thanks for letting us know right away. I can't wait to tell Billy."

Squirrel hung up the phone and looked at me, grinning like the Cheshire cat. "You'll never guess what Emma found out about the cat lady."

"So what did she say?"

"Skip and some of the staff at the paper did a deep dive into the 'tombs.' It turns out the cat lady was Olive Mackey, Noah Mackey's daughter. The house was originally built by a man who made his fortune in the shipping business. When Noah died in 1950, Olive bought it on the q.t. and left Noah's place on the island. Apparently she's lived there ever since."

"You think this is our Olive?"

"It must be. Emma thinks so, that's for sure. She said they're still working the story, trying to get it out for the morning edition. There might be more, she said. Whatever they find, it'll end up in the paper."

"Wow," I said, "that's really something. It's too bad we didn't find out sooner."

"Yeah, we could have given her the pendant, maybe gotten her to tell us the real story behind it."

"Probably too late for that now," I said.

"Maybe not. Let's see what the folks at the newspaper come up with."

When the morning chores were done and we were back in the house, Squirrel said, "Why don't you go fish the paper out of the ditch while I fix breakfast."

Our newspaper delivery was spotty, depending on who was working the route. The little bridge that connected our driveway to the road was the main problem. It spanned the drainage ditch that ran beside the road. Most carriers didn't slow down much as they tossed the rolled up paper out the window or over the top of their car, and they didn't bother to see where it landed. If they timed it right, the paper ended up on the edge of the driveway. If not, it was likely to end up in the ditch. One kid, who rode a motorcycle, was especially good at putting the paper in the ditch most of the time. Once, when he was delivering the bigger Sunday paper, the rubber band holding the paper together broke in midair, and the pages went flying all over the place.

We'd mostly solved the problem by getting one of those metal tubes and attaching it to the post below the mailbox. Emma got it for us, a yellow tube with the *Herald* logo stenciled in blue on the side. The bright yellow was hard to miss, even in the dark, but some of the carriers still tossed the paper at the driveway anyway.

I was optimistic about finding the paper. Our current carrier, Elsie Hanlin, was a retired school bus driver, and she hadn't let us down very often. I wanted to see what they had to say about Olive, the cat lady, without having to poke around in the ditch. Sure enough, when I got to the bridge, I saw the rolled up paper peeking out of the tube. I tucked it under my arm and headed back to the house.

Squirrel had made a fresh pot of coffee and was dishing up plates of scrambled eggs when I came into the kitchen.

She put a toasted English muffin on each plate and carried the plates over to the table.

I sat down, slipped off the rubber band, and unrolled the paper to take a look. "I don't see anything on the front page."

Squirrel spread some butter on her muffin. She paused, her knife in midair. "It's probably not a front page story. Look in the B section."

"That's a good idea. Give me a second." I buttered my muffin, spread a little jelly on top, and wiped my hands on a napkin before separating the newspaper sections. The B section was where the local news stories appeared.

The headline was hard to miss: " 'Cat Lady' Olive Mackey, dies at 85." There was a photo of the mansion under the picture, apparently taken when the place was in its heyday. The garden was well tended, and there was a fancy car parked in the driveway.

Squirrel put on her reading glasses and pulled the paper closer. "Let me see," she said.

I took a bite of my muffin as Squirrel started reading the article.

"Olive Mackey, only child of Noah Mackey, pioneer lumber baron and community benefactor, died of natural causes in her home on J Street. The elaborate mansion was built in 1890 by shipping magnate J. R. Hargrove, who amassed a considerable fortune in the early days on Heron Bay. Upon his retirement in 1950, Hargrove moved to San Francisco. Following Mr. Mackey's death that same year, his daughter left her father's home on the bay island bearing his name and moved into the Hargrove house on J St."

"Interesting stuff," I said. "Does it say anything more about Olive?"

"It just says how she became reclusive in her later years, supposedly living alone in the house with only her cats to keep her company, a rumor that turned out to be just gossip. It says there was only one cat found on the property, and none in the house at all."

"I guess if a story gets told often enough, everyone will start to believe it. Anything else?"

"The article talks about the grounds surrounding the house. Apparently she had a full-time gardener who kept everything just so, but he disappeared sometime in the eighties. Folks figured she'd just run out of money and couldn't afford to keep the place up."

I started working on my eggs, which were turning cold. "So what happens to the place now?" I asked.

"They don't know yet. It says the terms of her will have not been released."

A couple hours later, we drove into town to pick up some things at Olsen's. Dean was in the office, and we spent a few minutes chatting with him about the fair. He'd made a lot of sales at the fairgrounds and seemed pretty pleased. He asked us about our 4-H group, and we told him about the new members we hoped to sign up and gave him a rundown on how the kids had done this year.

We ordered what we needed, paid Dean, and went out to the warehouse to pick up our supplies. The young man we'd seen last time helped us again, stacking our feed sacks on a hand truck and wheeling them out to the dock. I opened the trunk, and he stepped down off the dock to put them in the car. We thanked him, and he headed back inside.

I drove out to the street, intending to get back on the highway, but Squirrel had another idea. "Why don't we drop by the *Herald* and see if Emma found out anything else?"

I thought about that for a second. "Well, I'm as curious as you are, but I don't know how much more there is to tell."

"You might be right, but not everything gets into the papers."

"True enough," I said, thinking of what we'd learned on our own. I pulled out onto the street and headed downtown.

We passed by the old mansion as we drove down J Street to the end of the block and the office of the *Herald*. There weren't any parking places in front of Emma's place, so we took a spin around the block and ended up finding a space further up the block, directly in front of the cat lady's house—Olive's house, as we'd found out. We sat there a moment, looking at the sad façade.

Squirrel released her seat belt and reached down to pick her purse up from the floor, preparing to step out. When I looked over to make sure she was ready, I saw some movement at the door of the house. The door opened, and a woman stepped out, carrying something in her hand. It was Earlene.

"Look," I said, pointing.

Squirrel looked toward the house. "That's Earlene. What's she doing here?"

As we watched, Earlene closed the door behind her, then turned and hung the black wreath she'd had in her hand on the door.

29

When Squirrel and I got out of the car and closed the doors, Earlene turned, looking toward the street. She hesitated when she saw us, and I thought for a moment she was going to go back inside. Instead, she came down the steps and headed our way, stopping just inside the gate.

"I'm surprised to see you here," she said.

"Emma told us what happened. It was in the paper this morning. We were planning to visit her at the *Herald*." Earlene looked guilty, like she'd been caught in a lie, but that wasn't really true. She hadn't lied. She just hadn't told us everything she knew.

"I guess you figured out who Olive was when you read the story in the paper," she said.

"Yeah," Squirrel said. "The article made it pretty clear. We were going to see if Emma had any more to tell us."

"Everything people need to know came out in the paper. All that stuff about the old lady who lived in the house with her cats." Earlene turned back and looked at the house. When she looked at us again, her shoulders slumped, and she had a resigned expression on her face. "Of course, there's more to the story. You probably figured that out, too."

"That's why we were going to see Emma," I said.

"They don't know everything over there at the *Herald*." Earlene frowned and looked down at the ground for a moment. When she looked up again, she said, "I've kept things from you because of a promise I made a long time ago, but I suppose that doesn't matter now. Come inside, and I'll explain everything."

Earlene unlocked the gate and let us inside, closing the

gate behind us. We followed her across the overgrown yard to the house, which wasn't quite as impressive close up as it looked from the street. Gray stucco walls with ivy climbing up nearly to the red tile roof flanked an elaborate portico with white-painted columns on either side of the front door. The paint on the columns and window trim was peeling away. Protected from the weather by the roof over the porch, the arched double doors of the entry were in better shape, the varnished oak still golden. The windows in the doors and sidelights were curtained, blocking the view to the interior.

Earlene took a key ring from her pocket and unlocked the front door, holding it open for us as we stepped inside. She closed the door and switched on the light, an elegant chandelier that hung below an ornate plaster medallion on the high ceiling. A long hallway with intricate parquet flooring stretched ahead of us, with rooms opening on either side.

The room on the right was fitted out as an office, complete with a library table and bookcases on either side of a Wooton desk against the back wall. Earlene led us into a formal parlor on the left.

"Most of the furniture in the front rooms came with the house," Earlene said when she saw us taking it all in.

Dark green wallpaper in a floral pattern covered the walls. A fainting couch with mohair and tapestry upholstery rested beneath the front window, the floral tapestry faded from the light. A table beside it held a bronze lamp with a leaded glass shade. A fireplace on the outside wall was decked out with an elaborately carved redwood mantel and a beveled glass mirror above it.

Two upholstered settees with button-tufted backrests faced each other near the fireplace. There was a low, marble-topped table between them. Earlene sat on one of the settees and pointed to the other.

"Have a seat," she said. "It's a long story."

I sat carefully on the settee, its spindly legs not inspiring confidence. Squirrel settled in beside me, apparently not concerned.

Earlene looked at me and smiled. "Don't worry, Billy. These old things are stronger than they look. The horsehair padding leaves a lot to be desired, but it won't fall apart under you."

Earlene looked down at her hands folded in her lap. We waited a few moments as she sat across from us—composing her thoughts, I supposed.

"When I saw Olive's name on that silver box," she said, looking up, "and you told me where you found it, I knew how it came to be there."

Squirrel looked at Earlene, waiting. "But there's more to the story, of course."

Earlene gave a hint of a smile, "Isn't there always?

"When you came to the office, we talked about how the older generation kept secrets and how rich people don't like to air their dirty linen in public. I mentioned how my father told me a lot I didn't know about our family history."

"I remember," I said. "It made me wonder what Ollie told you."

"My father wasn't very talkative. He took care of our place, taught me how to do things, but he didn't say much about how he felt inside. I never knew my mother. She left when I was really little. Dad just said she didn't take to living back in the hills, and ran off, looking for a bigger pond to fish in. I think that was part of his reluctance to talk about things."

Earlene looked away for a moment, then turned back to look at us. "I think there was some shame in it, too. Families have their secrets, and sometimes it's just easier to keep them buried—not pass that burden on to the next generation, you know?"

I glanced at Squirrel. I could tell she was thinking it over. She looked at Earlene and nodded. I thought I knew where Earlene was going, but I wasn't sure. I wanted to hear it from her.

"It all goes back to Noah Mackey, that pillar of the community everybody thinks so highly of." She paused again before continuing. "It turns out he had an Indian mistress he was sleeping with. When she got pregnant, he wouldn't have anything to do with the child. Sleeping with her was okay, but he certainly wasn't going to marry her, even though Olive's mother had died young. He was happy to put his name on everything he touched, but after the baby came, he didn't want to have anything to do with either of them."

"So, what happened?" I asked.

"Mackey bought the woman's silence, moved her and the baby to the farm in the hills above Prairie Creek... the farm where I grew up."

Squirrel looked my way. "You mean...?"

"Yeah. She named the baby Ollie after his half-sister and took the name Mack to spite Noah."

I looked over at Squirrel who seemed as surprised as I was. "So you're saying..."

"That son of a bitch was my grandfather, and his daughter Olive was my aunt."

"Wow," Squirrel said. "So you didn't know any of this till Ollie let you in on the family history?"

"No. Like I said, I think there was some shame in it, somehow. Plenty of that to go around."

I tried to imagine how Earlene felt when Ollie told her Noah Mackey was her grandfather. "All that must have come as quite a shock," I said.

"That's for sure," Earlene said. "Anyway, all that's in the past." She paused for a moment. "But the past has a way of catching up with us. When I saw the name on the box and saw the pendant, I knew what it was right away, but I promised to keep Aunt Olive's story private as long as she was alive."

"Like you said," Squirrel offered, "everything people need to know came out in the paper."

"I'd like to keep it that way. Aunt Olive was good to me, tried to make up for her old man's shortcomings. She inherited a lot of money when he died, used a lot of it to promote Indian causes and help renovate the Mackey building for the cultural center. Most people think all that money came from the casino, but it didn't."

We sat there for a minute or two, thinking about what she'd said. It was a lot to take in. Finally, Squirrel and I told Earlene what we'd found out about Jacob and what we thought they were doing on the south jetty that night.

"You probably saw the special edition the *Herald* put out celebrating their 150 year anniversary," I said. "There was a picture in the article with Mackey and his daughter up on the Klamath. Emma found the original picture in the paper's archives. The photographer wrote the names on the back of the photo, identifying Jacob as Noah's river guide. We figured it out from there."

"I thought you'd get around to that sooner or later," she said. "I remember how you and Pepper figured out what went on at the old lumber camp. I expected to see you at the fair, but then Aunt Olive got sick, and I needed to be with her. She was the only family I had left."

"We did wonder where you were," I said. Doris just told me something had come up that needed your attention."

"Doris is a good friend. She knew where I was, but I knew she wouldn't say anything."

She looked away for a moment, then turned back. "Anyway, that's all behind us now. Jacob is the rest of the story, and I guess you might as well hear it from me." Earlene stood up then, pointing toward the hallway. "Let's take a walk."

We followed Earlene down the long hallway. On the left, a staircase led upstairs. A leaded glass window on the landing cast some light on the parquet floor. We headed toward the back of the house, passing by doors opened to other rooms, a back parlor with a television on a stand and more modern, comfortable-looking chairs, and what appeared to be the original dining room, with a hospital bed where the dining table once stood.

At the end of the hall, Earlene slid open a pocket door that led into the kitchen, a no-nonsense space where servants originally prepared meals. It was all business: embossed tin ceiling, a gas range with enameled oven doors, a farm sink, and a work table with a stainless steel surface.

We passed through the kitchen and the laundry room behind it to the back door, finding ourselves in a covered breezeway between the main building and the carriage house. The breezeway opened on one side to the alley that separated the property from the *Herald* building.

A path on the other side led into the overgrown garden.

Earlene sat down on a stone bench at the edge of the path and patted the seat beside her. Squirrel sat beside her, looked my way. The bench wasn't big enough for the three of us. I gave them a "you go ahead" wave and leaned up against the wall of the carriage house.

"Aunt Olive told me what happened on the beach that night. As you figured out, Olive met Jacob when her father hired him as a river guide on his fishing trips. He was her age, handsome as hell, and Olive was quite taken with him. They got to know one another while her old man went off drinking with his cronies at the end of the day. Mackey was furious when he found out what was going on behind his back. It was okay for him to cozy up with his Indian lover, but by God, he wasn't gonna let 'one of them red niggers' get near his daughter. He did everything he could to keep them apart, kept Olive in that house on the island most of the time.

"As you can imagine, Jacob and Olive managed to find ways to see each other from time to time. When Jacob went off to the war, Olive's father thought that was the end of it. Their love was on hold, but they kept in touch with letters. When Jacob came home, they got together again. Whenever Olive could get away, they would slip off together for a few hours. That was how they ended up on the south jetty that night."

"So Mackey got wind of it?" Squirrel asked.

"Yeah. He had people following her all the time. Someone tipped him off, and he drove out there with two thugs he hired, and they beat Jacob, left him for dead, and hauled Olive back to Mackey island."

Squirrel shuddered. "What a horrible man."

"What about the pendant?" I asked.

"Aunt Olive told me about it. She said Jacob gave it to her that night on the beach. It was supposed to be an engagement gift. When Mackey saw her clutching it in her hand, he ripped it away from her and threw it out the window as they drove away from the beach.

"I'd never seen it, of course, but when I saw Olive's name on the silver box, I knew it must be what Jacob gave her that night."

We sat there for a minute or two, not knowing what to say.

Ollie's revelations had hit Earlene hard, but it was nothing compared to what Olive and Jacob had been through.

Earlene looked down the path to the garden. A white butterfly flitted between the bushes lining the path, rose on the breeze, and disappeared in the tangle beyond.

Earlene looked my way, saw me leaning against the wall. "Did you see the picture in this morning's paper, the one of the house with that fancy car in the drive?"

"Yeah, looked like it was taken a long time ago."

"That was Noah's town car, a '41 Hollywood Graham he bought new right before the war to show off his wealth. He kept it garaged in a warehouse he owned down by the docks, drove it everywhere. When he died, Aunt Olive sold the warehouse, and the car ended up here. She never learned to drive—Mackey didn't believe women should drive cars."

Earlene stood up and fished the key ring out of her pocket. "After what happened on the beach, she didn't want to have anything more to do with that car. The big black monstrosity's been in the carriage house ever since."

Earlene inserted a key in the lock, turned it, and opened the door. "Take a look if you want," she said.

Squirrel walked over, and we went inside. It was dark in there, but I found a light switch beside the door. A bare bulb hanging from the rafters lit up the space, revealing the old car covered in a layer of dust.

Earlene was right. It was a monster. It had a long, coffin-shaped hood, fender-mounted headlights, and lots of chrome in the bumper and grill. The windshield was slanted, and the roof curved toward the rear like the swept-back fenders on the sides of the car. The tires were flat, and the wide whitewalls had cracked from age. One of the hubcaps was missing. I figured I knew where the other one was.

We went back outside, closing the door behind us. Earlene

was sitting on the bench.

"That's quite the car," I said. "A collector would pay a lot for an old car like that."

Earlene looked up. "I know—and they're welcome to it. Aunt Olive didn't want to have anything to do with it, and I don't either."

I thought about what Earlene said. Olive's father had driven her away from the beach in that car, leaving Jacob for dead. I could understand how she felt about it. "So what happened to Jacob?" I asked.

"Like I said earlier, Jacob's the rest of the story."

30

Earlene locked the door to the carriage house and pocketed the key. We followed as she led us along the path into the overgrown garden. She paused and turned our way, then pointed toward the street where we'd parked our car, now impossible to see behind the tangle of bushes that had spread everywhere.

"You saw the picture in the paper—the way the garden used to look?"

"Yeah," Squirrel said. "It was beautiful."

"That was mostly Jacob's doing. He had help in the beginning. There were servants in the house and others who kept up the building, but the grounds were what Jacob enjoyed most."

Earlene led us around the corner of the house, past a side porch with wide steps that let into the garden. The path was bordered by low boxwood hedges, now untrimmed and tangled.

We stopped to look around. "It must have been lovely," Squirrel said.

"I remember driving by when we were kids," I said. "That was back in the fifties. Everything still looked pretty nice from the street."

"I saw it back then, too, "Earlene said. "Everything was trimmed and clipped just so. It was very formal-looking."

"Not very welcoming, though," I said. "Unless you were coming to a party, and parking your fancy car in the driveway."

"When Hargrove built the house, he gave lots of parties for his friends and business associates, but Aunt Olive and

Jacob weren't like that. They pretty much kept to themselves."

We walked on toward the back of the property. The fence at the front was a low stuccoed wall, with wrought iron above it, but the wall at the rear was over six feet tall, making for a very private space back here.

"Of course," Earlene said, "they made their own life together." She paused where the path branched off, leading to an outbuilding that was nearly covered with ivy—a garden shed, I supposed. A gated opening in the wall behind the shed led to the street that passed behind the property. Probably for deliveries, I thought.

"Mostly, they preferred their own company, at least in town. But Aunt Olive told me they had a cabin up on the Trinity River. They spent a lot of time up there, especially in the summer, when the weather was good and they could get away from the coastal fog and overcast days. Jacob's Hupa friends and the people he knew from his time on the Klamath would come down to visit, and they had a lot of fun."

"How'd they get up there?" I asked.

"Certainly not in Noah's old car," Earlene said, giving me a frowny look. "Aunt Olive never learned to drive, but Jacob always had a car—kept it in that shed," she said, pointing. "It was usually a little Ford sedan, plain-looking, but good enough to get around town and take them to the cabin in the summer."

Squirrel looked at Earlene, smiled. "Sounds like they had a pretty good life, but certainly a quiet one. They didn't have any children?"

"Aunt Olive told me there was a baby, but it only lived a few days. They never had another. She and Jacob were never married, and she worried that folks would label any child of theirs a 'half-breed bastard'—her words, not mine."

I cringed when I heard that. "We've come a long ways

since then, I think."

Earlene frowned at me. "Depends on whose moccasins you're walkin' in. I get plenty of stares when I'm on the street. But you're right—things are better than they were back then. Folks who find out they've got some Native blood don't try to hide it like they used to."

Earlene continued down the path, away from the shed where Jacob had kept their car. She headed toward the back corner of the property, furthest away from the house. Small trees, crepe myrtles, maybe, grew along the walls, forming a shady nook in the corner where the walls met. The bushes on either side were waist-high, and dandelions had sprung up in the gravel path, yellow blossoms rising above the green leaves. A magnificent thistle with spiky purple blooms leaned out over the path. We pulled our arms in and stepped single file around it.

"So what happened to Jacob?" I asked. Squirrel put her hand on my arm, giving me a look.

Earlene turned and gave us that resigned look we'd seen earlier. "Jacob died in '86," she said. "Aunt Olive said he'd been working in the garden that day. After dinner, he told her he wasn't feeling well and went to lie down. When she went in to check on him later, he was gone."

"That must have been a terrible shock," Squirrel said.

"Yeah. Jacob was only in his sixties. They should've had more time together."

"You never know," I said lamely.

"Aunt Olive told me she kind of fell apart when Jacob died, stopped caring about things, you know? She sold off the cabin on the Trinity, wouldn't see any of their friends, just withdrew into herself."

"Jacob was everything to her," Squirrel said.

"Yes. They were everything to each other." Earlene

looked away. A gust of wind stirred the leaves in the trees up ahead. After a moment, she turned back toward us. "After a while, she let the servants go. She could fend for herself, but she didn't care about the house any more."

"She just stayed in the house by herself?" I asked.

"Yeah, that's when the stories started about the crazy old lady who lived here with her cats. I don't know who started it, but it gave people something to talk about."

"We all heard those stories when we were growing up," Squirrel said.

"Me, too," Earlene said. "I thought they were true, like everyone else. I had no idea the cat lady was my aunt—my father's sister."

"Must have been quite a surprise," I said.

"Yeah. But there were other surprises. When I decided to get in touch with my heritage and started working at the cultural center, I knew we had an anonymous benefactor, but nobody there would say who it was. When my father told me that the cat lady was his sister, I still didn't know. When I found out eventually, it made sense. Aunt Olive was using Noah's money to make up for what happened to Jacob and others."

The path ahead curved toward the crepe myrtles in the corner. As we rounded the curve, Earlene stopped and turned to look at us. "Aunt Olive was a good person. Her father was a hateful man, but she cared about others. Most of all, she cared about Jacob."

Earlene stepped aside, pointing toward the trees. "Go ahead. Take a look."

Squirrel and I looked at each other, unsure what Earlene wanted to show us. We walked along the gravel path, Earlene trailing behind. Neither of us were prepared for what we saw when we rounded the curve.

The path ended in an open circle bordered by plants, but these weren't the overgrown shrubs we'd seen everywhere else. The circle was lined with blue-and-white forget-me-nots, carefully shaped into low mounds. Behind them, purple asters were covered with daisy-like blossoms with yellow centers. Ferns grew in the shade beyond them.

Squirrel and I stood there, taking it all in. It was stunning, a secret garden so different from the rest of the yard. Earlene came up behind us, sitting on another stone bench at the edge of the path.

Like the path, the open area was paved with gravel, but here it was carefully raked and free of weeds. A purple gazing ball on a concrete stand stood in the center of the circle.

I looked at Squirrel as she took it all in. Earlene came up beside us, her footsteps crunching on the gravel. "This is really something," I said.

"Look in the middle," she said, pointing toward the gazing ball.

Squirrel and I stepped into the center. A gray stone was set into the ground there. It had a design resembling the ones we'd seen on those baskets in the museum carved into the border. In the center was the letter J—nothing else.

Squirrel took my arm, leaning her head on my shoulder. "Aw… Billy…" she said.

Earlene looked at the stone, then across the way, where another of those white butterflies danced along the line of forget-me-nots. "This was Aunt Olive's special place. She spent a lot of time here—'with Jacob,' she told me. The rest of the yard might go to ruin, but she made sure to take care of this part."

I thought about what we'd seen. I asked Earlene how Olive had managed to have Jacob buried on the property. I didn't think you could do that.

"Money and influence can make a lot of things happen. My grandfather got away with a lot—used his money to cover his sins. Aunt Olive put her money to better use."

I remembered what Earlene told us about Olive's support of Indian causes and her part in the renovation of the Mackey building. It wasn't too hard to see how she might have managed to keep Jacob with her.

Squirrel sat on the bench with Earlene. "So what will happen now?" she asked.

"Aunt Olive provided for me, but the house and its contents will be sold. She's leaving everything to various Native causes—some to support the work of the cultural center, a scholarship program for Hupa youth, job training programs, those kinds of things."

"The house is sitting on half a block close to downtown," I said. "It must be worth a lot."

Earlene glanced back toward the house, a wistful half-smile on her face. "I imagine so." She paused, thinking for a moment. "It will go a long way, but I'll always miss her. She was my last living relative."

Squirrel turned her head toward the grave. "What about Jacob?"

"Aunt Olive provided for him, too."

31

It was a cool October morning, the gray overcast beginning to burn off as the sun rose above the tide flats on the eastern end of Heron bay. Earlene had invited us to join her for the opening ceremony of the newly created memorial on Mackey Island, now renamed Indian Island, as she had predicted.

Earlene was waiting on the dock when Squirrel and I arrived.

The tide was in, and the *Minchin*, the small boat that provided bay tours for locals and tourists, rubbed gently against the bumpers lining the dock. Today the blue-and-white boat was shuttling visitors to the island for the celebration. The *Minchin* only carried a dozen or so people at a time, seated fore and aft of the cabin in the center, so it would be making several trips.

The ship's pilot, dressed in a pea coat and a navy blue watch cap, welcomed us aboard and told us to sit where we liked. The three of us chose a spot along the rail behind the cabin, and the others who had been waiting on the dock with Earlene filled in the remaining seats.

When everyone was settled, the deckhand cast off the mooring lines. The pilot sounded a blast on the boat's horn, gunned the motor, and the *Minchin* swung away from the dock, heading across the bay. Diesel smoke from the pipe above the cabin drifted our way, mixing with the sour smell from the pulp mill on the north jetty. Sea gulls wheeled overhead, following the ship's foamy wake. The sturdy boat plowed steadily along in spite of the slight chop on the water created by the morning breeze.

It was only a mile or so to the island in the middle of the bay. The tour boat wasn't built for speed, but even so, it wouldn't take long to get to the island. I nodded at Squirrel, gave her a questioning look. "Go ahead," I said.

Squirrel reached into her pocket and took out the silver box. Earlene was looking out across the bay toward the island. Squirrel touched her sleeve to get her attention. "We brought you something," she said.

Earlene turned away from the view and saw what Squirrel had in her hand. "It's yours, now," Squirrel said, handing it to her. "We thought you might want to wear the pendant for the ceremony."

Earlene looked at the box, ran her fingers over the design on top.

"Thank you," she said. She opened the box and took out the pendant, holding it up. "Lovely, isn't it?" She stared at it for a moment, turning it one way and another. "Aunt Olive would have loved it."

"It's too bad we couldn't have returned it to her," Squirrel said, "but we know how much it will mean to you."

Earlene slipped the chain over her head, letting the pendant rest below the collar of her shirt. She held it in one hand, rubbing her thumb over the smooth onyx stones. When she looked up at us, there was a sparkle in her eyes—a tear welling up, I thought. "Thanks again," she said. "You're right. It means a lot to me."

The memorial building came into view as we neared the island. It was a low structure with a peaked roof. The wide overhang in front was supported by peeled redwood poles, and the front wall was adorned with the great seals of the local tribes, the same ones we'd seen when we visited the cultural center downtown. An antique redwood dugout canoe leaned against the wall at one end.

The ceremonies were well underway when we arrived. A steady throbbing drumbeat and chanting voices drowned out the purr of the diesel engine as the pilot swung the boat around to tie up at the pier. Women in ceremonial regalia, like the shell dresses we'd seen in the museum, danced in the open space in front of the building as the visitors gathered around them looked on.

The gangplank was lowered, and we followed the other passengers onto the pier. We climbed the wooden stairs at the other end, joining the crowd surrounding the dancers in the open area in front of the memorial building.

The dancing continued for quite a while as we watched. With the pulsing beat of the drums, the jingling of the shell dresses, and the steady chanting, it was easy to get caught up in the intensity of the celebration that meant so much to the local Indians.

As we looked on, a group of women came out from the memorial building. Squirrel pointed in their direction. I recognized Doris among them. She stepped up to a podium that was set up on the porch.

Earlene saw the women, too. "Doris is going to make the dedication speech today," she said. "She's been a good friend, cares as much as I do about the work we do at the Center, maybe more. She's been there since the beginning. When I told her what my father said about our family history, that was when she told me Aunt Olive was our anonymous benefactor."

"That must have come as quite a surprise," I said.

Earlene looked at me, smiled. "Kind of—but it made a lot of sense. It's just what my aunt would do, to honor Jacob and make up for her father's wrongdoings."

"Sounds complicated," Squirrel said.

"I asked Doris about the arrangement, but she didn't give me all the details. She just said, 'We have an Indian lawyer—a good one.'"

When the dancing ended, Doris stepped up to the podium and looked out over the crowd, waiting for them to settle. She thanked everyone for coming, enlisting a round of applause when she introduced the dancers. She spoke of the determination and hard work that led to the creation of the memorial. She spoke at some length about the island's history and the massacre that had taken place more than a century ago, "our native blood staining the land we now reclaim and dedicate to a higher purpose." She said the intertribal memorial was created to celebrate Native history and culture and to assure that "those who rest here will not be forgotten."

It was a powerful speech. I glanced at Squirrel. She made a sniffling sound and looked at me, wiping away a tear with the back of her hand. Earlene had that same teary sparkle in her eyes I'd seen earlier.

Doris thanked everyone again for coming to the dedication and invited them to tour the exhibits in the memorial building. People began to drift toward the entrance, but there were too many to enter at one time, and a line formed outside.

"Let's not wait," Earlene said. "We can see the exhibits later, when the line isn't so long. I want to show you something."

The morning overcast was gone and the sky overhead was clear. The wind had eased up, but there was still a fall chill in the air. Earlene led us along a path that went around the side of the building to a large open area behind it. A stand of tall Monterey cypress trees grew on the north side of the island, the smokestack of the pulp mill visible beyond it. White birds perched in the trees and circled above. "My grandfather planted those trees," Earlene said. "Supposed to be a windbreak. Now they're home to the herons and egrets."

Most of the land behind the memorial building was covered with grass. We followed along a path not far from the water's edge, where the spiky grass was shorter and easier to navigate.

"This was Wiyot land for ages," Earlene said. She pointed across the open area. "Their village was here. The victims of the massacre and the bones of their ancestors are here, too."

Earlene stepped into the taller grass, walking toward a small fir tree that had sprung up in the grass. She stopped beside the little tree. The grass was shorter here, and the ground looked like it had been recently disturbed.

Earlene fingered the pendant in her right hand and pressed it to her chest. "They're all here," she said. "Under the grass. Jacob and Olive, too."

Squirrel took my arm and leaned against my shoulder as we thought about what Earlene was telling us. "Together again," I managed. I remembered a few lines from the Carl Sandburg poem: "I am the grass; I cover all... Shovel them under and let me work."

Earlene looked up, turned toward the memorial building behind us. "Aunt Olive grew up here in that monstrous house her father built. It's gone now, but Olive's come back to stay— she and Jacob. She's home now. It was what she wanted."

As we stood there, taking it all in, another line from the poem came to mind: "Two years, ten years... what place is this?" Sandburg was probably right. People forget. But we would remember.

32

After the apples had been picked and the kids' pumpkins had been made into pies and jack-o'-lanterns, Squirrel and I had a little time to relax. One evening after dinner, the phone rang. It was Emma, calling to tell us the *Herald* had bought the property next door. The paper was going to expand, creating new office space and updating the plant. Plans were underway to demolish the cat lady's place and replace it with a new office building. She knew how important the old place had become to us and figured we'd want to know right away.

She was right, of course. It was inevitable, but sad, too. The demolition was set to begin in a couple of weeks. She promised to let us know when it started.

"Emma doesn't know the whole story, does she?" I asked.

"Only what was in the newspaper," Squirrel said.

"Earlene said everything people needed to know came out in the paper, didn't she?"

"I remember." She paused, a serious look on her face. "Maybe we should keep it that way."

We joined the small crowd that lined the walk in front of Olive's former home. It was a chilly November morning, overcast and damp. The demolition was already underway. The surrounding fences and walls had been taken down, hauled away days before. The palm trees and the overgrown shrubbery were gone, pushed into a pile by the yellow Caterpillar tractor that squatted at the edge of the lot. The ground was scraped bare, now just brown dirt crisscrossed by the tracks of the bulldozer.

The tiles were gone from the roof, and an orange crane swung an iron wrecking ball back and forth, pounding away at the upper story. Men in hard hats scuttled here and there. A blue dump truck stood apart from the house, waiting to haul away the rubble.

Earlene and Doris came up the walk and stood beside us. We watched as the wrecking ball came down on the roof of the portico, knocking it to the ground. There were oohs and ahs from the others who'd gathered to watch, but we didn't say anything. It was the end of something we didn't have words for.

I thought about Jacob and Olive as we watched the house being torn apart. It was the end of their story—a love story their hearts had written and kept alive in spite of what the world threw at them. I looked at Squirrel standing beside me, and took her hand in mine. We'd had an easier time of it, but we were writing a love story of our own just the same. Earlene and Pepper hadn't fared so well. I thought of Teddy and Dolly then, still working on the first chapters of their story. I hoped it had a happy ending.

Acknowledgments

My thanks to Eileen Crowley, my loyal first reader, for her kind comments and helpful suggestions; to fellow writers Gary Durbin and Kitty Fassett for their insights and suggestions that kept me on track throughout this project. And to Tim Jollymore and Finns Way Books for, as always, providing much-needed critical guidance and encouragement.

B. C.